Lord love her,
she'd never felt like this.

Gently, Glen's mouth covered hers, his tongue moving slowly, sensually, over her lips.

How good he tasted, of mint and coffee—and something else.

After the tender, hungry caress, he lifted his mouth from hers but still held her face in his hands.

"Now I know what Crane's Mountain Magic means," he whispered hoarsely.

"I told you," Laura murmured when she could, "I'm not part of the magic."

"For me you are."

Dear Reader,

Happy holidays! Though it may be cold outside, it's always warmed by the festivities of this special season. Everyone at Silhouette Books wishes you joy and cheer at this wonderful time of the year.

In December, we have some heartwarming books to take the chill off the weather. The final title in our DIAMOND JUBILEE celebration is *Only the Nanny Knows for Sure* by Phyllis Halldorson. Don't miss this tender love story about a nanny who has a secret . . . and a handsome hero who doesn't stand a ghost of a chance at remaining a bachelor!

The DIAMOND JUBILEE—Silhouette Romance's tenth anniversary celebration—is our way of saying thanks to you, our readers. To symbolize the timelessness of love, as well as the modern gift of the tenth anniversary, we've presented readers with a DIAMOND JUBILEE Silhouette Romance each month in 1990, penned by one of your favorite Silhouette Romance authors. It's been a wonderful year of love and romance here at Silhouette Books, and we hope that you've enjoyed our DIAMOND JUBILEE celebration. Saying thanks has never been so much fun!

And that's not all! There are six books a month from Silhouette Romance—stories by wonderful writers who time and time again bring home the magic of love. And we've got a lot of exciting events planned for 1991. In January, look for Marie Ferrarella's *The Undoing of Justin Starbuck*—the first book in the WRITTEN IN THE STARS series. Each month in 1991, we're proud to present readers with a book that focuses on the hero—and his Zodiac sign. Be sure to watch for that mysterious Capricorn man . . . and then meet Mr. Aquarius in *Man from the North Country* by Laurie Paige in February.

1991 is sure to be extra special. With works by authors such as Diana Palmer (don't miss her upcoming Long, Tall Texan!), Annette Broadrick, Nora Roberts and so many other talented writers, how could it not be? It's always celebration time at Silhouette Romance—the celebration of love.

I hope you'll enjoy this book and all of the stories to come. Come home to romance—Silhouette Romance—for always!

Sincerely,

Tara Gavin
Senior Editor

ADELINE McELFRESH

Crane's Mountain

Silhouette *Romance*

Published by Silhouette Books New York

America's Publisher of Contemporary Romance

SILHOUETTE BOOKS
300 E. 42nd St., New York, N.Y. 10017

ISBN: 0-373-08762-4

First Silhouette Books printing December 1990
Second Silhouette Books printing January 1991

Printed in the U.S.A.

Books by Adeline McElfresh

Silhouette Romance

ADELINE McELFRESH

lives in rural southern Indiana, where she pursues her dream—writing, reading, walking and generally enjoying life. She collects old medical books, early-American "home cures" and housekeeping hints. She is the author of numerous romance and suspense novels published under her own name and pseudonyms.

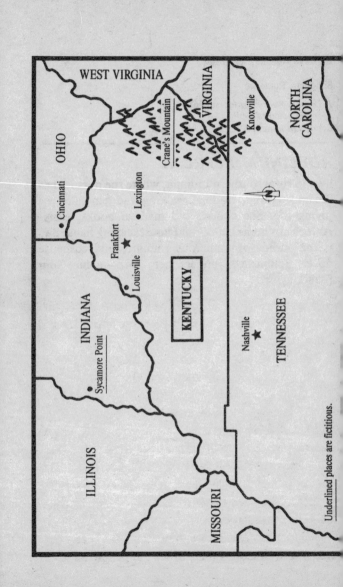

WEST VIRGINIA

OHIO

VIRGINIA

Crane's Mountain

Knoxville

NORTH CAROLINA

• Cincinnati

• Lexington

Frankfort ★

• Louisville

INDIANA

Sycamore Point

KENTUCKY

Nashville ★

TENNESSEE

ILLINOIS

MISSOURI

Underlined places are fictitious.

Prologue

Jolted awake, Glen Moran sat bolt upright, nearly spilling himself out of the hammock strung between two huge sycamore trees behind the rambling old house at Sycamore Point.

Damn nightmares. When would they stop?

Physicians, surgeons and physical therapists all the way from the near-primitive jungle hospital in Marazán to Georgetown University Hospital in Washington, D.C., had repaired his body and taught it to function again. The shrinks, however, hadn't done a heck of a lot for him; he still had recurring nightmares, though less frequently than at first.

Not to worry, he had been told. Go home, lie back, let nature take its course.

So, four months before, he'd done just that: come home to Sycamore Point, to let the people he loved and the kind of life he had longed for complete his healing.

Rubbing his hand over his face, he thought that nature was taking her own sweet time. He still needed a cane to walk. When he looked at himself—in the mirror as he shaved, and when he showered—the scars on his face, chest and left thigh reminded him just how close he'd come to buying that big newspaper in the sky.

Still, he sometimes smelled the stinking jungle muck when the wind was blowing in from the west bearing fragrances of spring along the Wabash River that separated southwestern Indiana from southeastern Illinois. Still, the sounds of gunfire and the exploding aircraft often haunted him when he woke in the dead of night.

This nightmare had been the first in three or four weeks, and he'd begun to think, hopefully, that he was through with them. Should have known better, he grumbled silently, dismissing such optimism. Some things a man's subconscious didn't forget, although his conscious mind usually managed to shove them onto a back shelf.

Lying back, he let his mind drift to another time, another place....

The jungle stretched beneath the low-flying plane like a seemingly endless, tranquil, dark green sea.

Nothing could be further from the truth, Glen Moran knew. Marazán, the small nation in Central America over which he and Frank Carrera were flying, hadn't known tranquility for two generations.

And the way things were going in the poverty-stricken land, anything but more violence and misery as the poor mestizos struggled to throw off economic and political oppression stemming largely from the country's illiteracy, seemed a long way off.

Leaning forward, Glen scanned the treetops again for a sign of the airstrip, which was the plane's destination. Either he or Carrera, the pilot, should have spotted it by now, for all that such makeshift "runways" hacked out of the jungle grew up again virtually overnight.

"Nothing," Carrera announced succinctly, without breaking the concentration of his search.

The knot in Glen's gut tightened.

If all had gone as planned, the landing strip should have been ready when the plane reached Marazán air space.

Obviously it wasn't.

Already they had crisscrossed and circled the key area twice. Continued survey at such a low altitude could prove dangerous. The drone of aircraft engines in the early-morning air over the silent jungle could attract a roving government patrol or a band of renegade guerrillas just as easily as it could bring the friendly laborers from the mission who would unload and transport the cargo.

There were times, Carrera had explained before takeoff in the States, when the best bet was to set down, unload, and then "get the hell off the ground."

This could well be one of them, Glen suspected.

Both sides in the undeclared Marazán conflict were so desperate for medicines and surgical supplies and equipment that they harassed the remote mission incessantly. In spite of the fact that the mission took care of all comers—soldiers and guerrilla rebels alike, as well as those who only wanted a better life for themselves and their families—they didn't care who ran the government. The mission was ripped off regularly.

"That would be Misión River."

Carrera pointed toward a thin blue thread that made a looping stitch in the green canopy that stretched as far as Glen could see before it plunged from sight, lost again in the dense tropical growth.

Glen swept his binoculars in the direction in which Carrera had pointed. Except for the brief dash of blue, the vegetation appeared unbroken, a carpet of sunlit greens in varying shades that would tell an old hand at jungle overflights like Frank Carrera what species of tropical flora they were crossing.

Not reassured, Glen focused on the point where the line of blue embroidery vanished into the sea of green.

He knew the Misión well. A beautiful, treacherous stream, the river ran through much of the Rhode Island-size nation, skirting the tiny church school and medical mission he had visited and written about on previous visits to Marazán.

Indians proud of their Spanish blood fished and swam in Misión River at considerable risk to life and limb. But the only traffic on the river—so narrow that, in places, branches linked with those from the other bank, and vines as thick as his arms looped across it— was small boats—very small boats, which also traveled at great risk, although from army and guerrilla patrols rather than from shallows and caimans.

"I'd feel better if it were half as wide as the Wabash back home." Keeping the binoculars on the scene below, Glen tried to wrench his mind off what might be hidden beneath the serene green cover. *"Not even you, my friend, can set this flying boxcar down in a crick like the Misión without busting the landing gear or taking off a wing."*

The plane was an army-surplus cargo craft of the Vietnam era, picked up for a song by the church organization that sponsored the mission.

"Relax, amigo." Carrera's soft, Spanish-accented voice was barely audible over the sound of the plane's twin engines. Carrera flew the craft as though he were a part of the plane. *"I have no more wish than you to become a meal for a hungry caiman."*

"It's not hungry caimans that worry me."

Glen kept his gaze on the green land beneath the wings. How could a place so beautiful harbor such misery? So much corruption and greed and violence?

"Sí."

Affirming the shared concern in his native tongue, the pilot brought his gaze back to the instrument panel. He was silent, his dark eyes studying the gauges for the span of a long breath.

"If we do not find our landing in the next five to ten minutes—" Glen could see him calculating the plane's rapidly dwindling fuel supply *"—we will air-drop as near to the compound as possible."*

They didn't dare break radio silence; Glen knew that. Nothing would bring an army or a guerrilla patrol—or both—quicker.

Although he didn't look forward to pushing all those supply crates out by himself, Glen nodded.

If they didn't spot the landing strip soon—and he had an idea Carrera was cutting it as close as he dared—they would have no choice but to take the chance that mestizos from the mission would find the supplies. After the long flight, the plane didn't carry enough fuel to make it to a friendly landing field outside Marazán with its heavy load.

Glen swore silently. His acting as copilot had made this flight his ticket into Marazán. His newspaper in Washington, D.C., had been told by Marazán authorities that neither he—especially—nor any other member of its staff would be welcome in the country. Glen's earlier exposé of Marazán's handling of U.S. aid funds, intended for the poor of the impoverished little nation, had infuriated General Mariana.

When the State Department had refused to intervene, he had started looking for other ways to get back into the country. Carrera's mercy flight fit the bill. He'd met Carrera three years ago and he respected, trusted and liked the man.

Born in Marazán's capital, Marazán City, Carrera now was a naturalized U.S. citizen who had enlisted in the United States Air Force at eighteen. By the time the Vietnam War began he had graduated from an accelerated college program and had become a hotshot pilot. A civilian now, he hired himself out and would fly anything with wings.

With luck, Glen had figured, he could melt into the jungle when the plane landed, and by the time the corrupt Marazán officials—and a couple of guerrilla leaders who were no better—learned he was there, he would have tracked down where the U.S. money was being funneled rather than being used to feed and clothe and educate the people who needed help. Juan Hernández, the Marazán newspaperman he had worked with before, would be expecting him.

If the plane was unable to land, he would have to start over. The story, he thought ruefully, had waited too long already.

"Amigo," Carrera began as he maneuvered the aircraft around for another pass over what should have been their target, "I know what you are feeling. My people need you to tell their story to the world more than the mission needs the medicines and the food we carry.

"But—" Something in Carrera's voice drew Glen's glance from the tropical flora below to the pilot's harsh profile. "I must tell you: I have this feeling that all is not well."

Glen let go the breath he had been holding without being aware of it until his lungs threatened to burst.

He also had "this feeling" about the landing and he didn't like the malaise that squiggled through him.

Long ago, he had learned to heed gut warnings—not that there was much he could do now about this one. Carrera was flying the plane in a tight spiral over the targeted area. Sunlight slanted into the dense growth at a different angle than it had earlier in the morning, revealing recesses in the forest that had been hidden from view in previous passes over the site.

Glen saw the slash in the vegetation at the same moment that Carrera shouted exultantly, "There it is! One o'clock!"

A narrow, dark gash in the rich, deep green seemed scarcely wider than a pencil. Men, who from the air appeared about the size of matchsticks, worked feverishly, swinging machetes whose blades glinted in the sunlight, to clear the way for the plane's landing.

"That—" Glen had to shout over the throb of the engines "—is what I call cutting it close."

The knot in his stomach loosened a little. Guessing that an army patrol or guerrillas had been in the area, and laborers from the mission had had to wait until the way was clear before beginning their task, he dragged a breath deep into his lungs and exhaled lustily. The tight ball of tension in his chest began to dissolve, although he would still feel its chill until his feet were once again on solid ground.

Out of the corner of his eye he caught the agate-hard glance Carrera shot him. "That is cutting it too close, amigo. Take another look."

With those words, the pilot shoved the throttle up. The plane's nose lifted, the twin engines sang a throatier song as increased power surged through them.

"We," Carrera yelled as he veered the craft sharply away from the runway, "are getting the hell out—"

The plane shuddered, then seemed to go into convulsions. Of its own accord, Glen's stomach did the same.

The big screen of Glen's mind had gone black again, like a TV when the program has been lost through some fluke. Sometimes it flickered, revealing bits and pieces of what was happening.

Sometimes, like now, there was nothing.

Glen shuddered. He was getting his life back together—but slowly, so slowly.

In the meantime, General Mariana was running amok and had been for too long. Power mad, the general was ripping off everything he could get his hands on and stashing it God knew where. And there were also the two guerrilla leaders who weren't much better. Juan Hernández had kept on feeding him information he couldn't publish in his own newspaper in Marazán City. The situation had only gotten worse in the last year and a half.

Regret slashed through Glen. Carrera had been a good man; a cool head in a crisis.

Glen could still hear the pilot's voice, softly Spanish-accented although he had lived in the United States since he was ten. "If you get out of this, amigo," Carrera had said, "and I do not see you again—" There had been a pause. "Write the story of my father and all the other good people of Marazán who have died trying to set their country free. Tell the world of the rape of my people by their own countrymen." His father had led an earlier army uprising against the Marazán government and when it failed, he had escaped with his family. After settling them in Texas, he had returned to Marazán, gone underground, and had been killed a few months later.

"When you have done that," Carrera had continued, "there is a lady named Laura Crane. Tell her she is the woman Frank Carrera would have liked to spend the rest of his life with."

A hard brown hand had then come off the unresponsive controls of the plane to grasp Glen's.

Now, his stomach clenching at the memory, Glen asked himself how many times he had said goodbye, good luck and Godspeed like that, with a handshake that had said it all.

It was time, he decided, as memory of the exploding plane and the crackle of gunfire from weapons in the hands of camou-garbed soldiers reverberated through his mind, to let someone else have the guts and the glory.

It was time to find Carrera's Laura Crane, deliver Carrera's message, and then wrap up the Marazán story and get out of the rat race.

"Comes a time, Moran," he muttered to himself, "when a man needs to fill that big void in his life with something besides a career."

Overhead, a blue jay that had been contemplating the scarcely moving hammock, squalled at the low rumble of words from the hammock's occupant.

Glen grinned and closed his eyes. He'd tell his sister, Laini, and D.J., her husband and his best friend—with whom he had dodged more bullets and ground-to-air and ground-to-ground missiles than he cared to recall as they'd covered brushfire wars and assorted other skirmishes in the Middle East and elsewhere—and Murphy, tonight. Murphy was the Mexican-American boy, now ten, whom Laini and D.J. had adopted when Glen had decided to return to D.C. to do the Marazán story.

Then, he would set about doing what he should have done a long time ago: replant his roots in Indiana soil where they belonged and start building the life he'd dreamed of—with a woman he could love and who would love him...give him children...help him instill in them the sense of values and family he'd grown up with.

But first, the Marazán story had to be told. He owed Carrera and too many other people down there.

Chapter One

Laura Crane woke with a feeling that today was going to be special.

A distinct sense of well-being seemed to surround her, suffuse her, tap into her soul. As though she'd been released from a dungeon, she felt a rush of warmth and a renewed zest for living such as she hadn't experienced in way over a year—in seventeen long months and twenty-three endless days and longer nights, to be exact. Two Christmases, usually her favorite time of year, had passed since she had been happy, since her spirit had felt alive.

It seemed like both an eternity and the day before yesterday.

This morning she even caught herself humming in the shower, a lilting little nothing of a tune, and when she dressed, she dug into her closet for a sheer wool sweater whose deep-blue color matched her eyes.

How long had it been since she'd paid attention to what she wore? *Before your world fell apart*, a little voice inside her answered, and she knew it was true. Anything went with jeans, her usual attire here on the mountain, and at the rare times when she'd gone off the mountain to show her sketches and paintings, it hadn't mattered to her what she wore.

She didn't understand why she felt different today.

Except for the season, nothing had changed for her since she'd learned of Frank's death, a few days before that Christmas of the year before last—the Christmas she didn't remember but knew she could never forget.

Why should this day early in June be the day when she felt at last as though life could be good again? Last June had been just as beautiful as this, she was sure, yet it was a blur in her memory.

Running a comb through chestnut hair that promptly cascaded over her shoulders as riotously as though the comb hadn't touched it, she stuck her bare feet into her moccasins and went out onto the deck that encircled the house.

A deep breath of the crisp morning air convinced her the day was for real.

Was it possible that the way she felt—almost exhilarated, as if she could spread imaginary wings and fly—was also real? *Could* her crushed spirit have healed even as she had mourned, without her having been aware what was happening?

She drew in another breath and held it, relishing its freshness in her lungs. Maybe all those well-meaning people who had assured her that time took the edge off even the sharpest grief were right.

But why was *today* the day she felt as though she might be ready at last to say goodbye to Frank and get on with her life without him? It was almost as if she sensed that something good was about to happen to her.

The wayward thought brought a whimsical smile to her lips. She didn't really believe in such nonsense, she chided herself.

The sun, barely up over the mountains, shone like red gold through a pale gray haze that would burn off as the morning progressed. Ribbons of fog hung in the treetops. A gentle breeze drifted across the deck, caressing her skin with its coolness.

Something magical seemed to be breathing on her, stirring tendrils of hair at her temples. The air, smelling of honeysuckle and damp earth, with just a tang of wood smoke that drifted up to her from her grandfather's store down the mountain, teased her senses.

This was nothing at all unusual. Enchantment abounded in the Cumberlands, if one were receptive to it.

The trouble was, lately—for nearly eighteen months—she hadn't felt the magic.

No, the change was in her: in her heart and in her soul, where for too long she'd felt only hurt and a bleak emptiness, as though she'd been trapped alone in some great, dark void, unable to find her way out into the sunlight.

Even yesterday had been like that, she mused. Loneliness had wrapped around her like a shroud.

She would love Frank always, would always revere his memory and miss him terribly. Forever she would feel that she and Frank could have had a wonderful life together if they'd only had the chance. And the time that had passed since his death had been one long nightmare reminding her it wasn't going to happen.

But somehow, without her having been conscious of its taking place, she had come to grips with her grief. Somehow she had accepted that her dream of becoming Frank's wife—or even his lover—wasn't going to come true.

Somehow she had learned to cope with her loss, had realized that the mountains around her were still beautiful, that the air she breathed was as pure and invigorating, the stars as bright, the moonglow as magic, as before.

She'd come to understand that she could treasure the rare times she and Frank had shared, that she could hold precious in her memory the love she'd felt for him...and been certain he'd felt for her, although he hadn't ever come right out and spoken the words she had wanted so badly to hear.

"Damn!"

The epithet exploded on her lips, the sound of it seeming blasphemous in the serenity of the morning.

Being a private person was fine and dandy—she was one, too; a woman who expressed herself best on sketch pad and canvas and was happiest when she was seated as motionless as a stone studying some wild creature she later would capture with pencil or brush. But Frank Carrera, she thought, had carried it too far.

So what if he had fought in what he had called "your father's war"?

Did that mean there was some law against telling her he loved her, asking her to marry him? Making love with her?

Frank Carrera had been right for her. Her heart and her mind had told her that. She had waited long enough for the right man, she'd told herself a few zillion times, to know him when she saw him.

A faint shift in the wind brought a stronger whiff of wood smoke, which in turn lured a smile to Laura's lips in spite of the pang that slashed through her. Grandpa Crane, Lord love him, thought he couldn't make coffee without firing up that old wood-burner down at the store, even in summer.

Glen Moran sat in the car for a couple of minutes, his arms folded on the wheel, and looked at the old storefront that reminded him of something in a Civil War movie.

Crane's General Mercantile
Groc., Hdwe. & Sundries
J. Crane, Esq. Est. 1837
Crane's Mountain, Ky.

The old codger already nodding off in a woven willow-bark chair, its sturdy frame peeled, seasoned and weathered through many seasons, might have been waiting for Jeb Stuart to ride by at the head of a column of Confederate cavalry—if, Glen mused, smiling inside, he wasn't J. Crane, Esq., come back to life in the body of a vintage mountain man.

Glen drew in a deep breath that, in spite of all the therapy and the time passed, still hurt his lungs. Finding Laura Crane hadn't been easy. Largely because of his slow recuperation from the injuries he had suffered in Marazán, he had delayed too long for his own peace of mind, letting Sycamore Point again weave its spell around him. The trip to Brownsville to see Carrera's sister had been long overdue by the time he'd gotten around to it a couple of weeks ago. Carmelita's not having a phone hadn't helped.

Now, to see if Laura Crane was here and deliver Carrera's message....

The pilot's last words to him crashed out of memory, ringing in his ears as they had so many times since he'd first heard them in those final moments before the plane had crashed into the end of the makeshift runway. Some of the times he'd heard it, he had been so nearly out of this world himself that he had wondered if he hadn't imagined the whole episode.

A lady named Laura Crane... Tell her she is the woman Frank Carrera would have liked to spend the rest of his life with.

Pain, prompted by that recollection and by the movement necessary to climb out of the car, shot through him.

For one sickening, frightening moment, he felt himself facedown again in that stinking, oozing jungle mud after the plane exploded and the Marazán army patrol moved in. He could almost feel the bullets again, slamming into his body and splattering in the mud around him...hear the exploding fuel tanks, feel the flames licking at him and the debris pelting his back.

He didn't know how he had gotten the few feet into the river, away from the burning fuel, or how he'd gotten out of the water and into a hut in the jungle where a terrified *mestizo* family had hidden him and kept him alive—barely.

Much later, he'd been told by one of the friendly guerrillas who had carried him—a step ahead of the pursuing patrol—how close he had come to dying before they had reached the guerrilla base hospital in the jungle. He had been a long time getting to a hospital in the States and then had spent nearly a year in one hospital after another, getting himself back together.

Finally discharged from Georgetown University Hospital, he had returned to Sycamore Point, to let the old homeplace restore his soul as the hospitals and doctors had restored his body.

After the crash, he'd learned that Carrera hadn't made it out of the plane. There had been precious little news out of Marazán since General Mariana's ironclad censorship had settled over the country like a blight.

Pulling himself together, he straightened, debated using the aluminum cane he'd ended up with but decided against it. He limped stiffly toward the wooden steps that led up to a wide-planked, unpainted porch that stretched across the front of the store.

"Morning," he said to the dozing old-timer when he had made his way laboriously up the steps, one hand holding on to the banister for dear life. The other clenched against the pain in his thigh.

The old man appeared to jerk awake.

"Eh?"

"Good morning. I'm looking for Laura Crane."

"Ain't here."

With the words, spoken in a gravelly wheeze, the whiskered chin dropped back toward the faded plaid shirt that was buttoned to a prominent Adam's apple.

Taking the hint, Glen thanked him and followed a strong aroma of coffee toward the screen door. Even before the terse response, he'd had little hope of finding Laura Crane inside. But the gallery whose name and Washington, D.C., address had been stamped on the back of a framed sketch of an eagle in flight that Carmelita Carrera Hosea had shown him had directed him to Crane's Mountain, Kentucky.

And this vintage store appeared to be Crane's Mountain, Kentucky—lock, stock and barrel.

Opening the screen door, he stepped inside, into an earlier century.

A cowbell over the door announced his passage.

"Feller inside is looking for you," the old man said when, a few minutes later, Laura ran lightly up the steps to the store's porch, most of it bathed in the early-morning sunshine.

The leggy black dog that ran with her flopped in a patch of shade and promptly closed his chocolate-brown eyes.

"Oh?" Laura cast a quick glance at the three- or four-year-old Buick parked near the gasoline pump but couldn't see the license plate from where she stood.

A vacationer down at the lake, most likely, she decided when she didn't recognize the car; someone who had heard that the little store near the lake hung a few Laura Crane originals that were for sale. Grandpa, Lord love him, prided himself on showing off her work. The knowledge made her smile. "Who?" she asked.

"Didn't say." The old man rubbed his whiskery chin with the back of one hand. "But he looks like he's been dragged through a knothole. Got a real bad limp and a scar on the side of his face, all the way across his temple. Thought he wasn't gonna git up them steps without taking a second hitch at it."

Laura's heart lurched into her throat. Frank!

Could it possibly be Frank, after nearly a year and a half?

"Thanks, Uncle Zeb."

Her heart felt as if it were three jumps ahead of her as she whirled toward the screen door.

The word from Marazán had been wrong!

Frank *had* survived the crash! He'd lost his memory, been held prisoner somewhere where he couldn't get word out to her, or some other equally terrible thing had happened to him!

It didn't matter. He had come back to her!

The cowbell above her head sounded the death knell for her soaring hopes as she jerked open the door and rushed inside.

As her heart crashed down from the mountaintop it had reached in record time, she willed herself to stop shaking. Inside, she felt sapped, drained of every scrap of energy, quivering and too weak to breathe.

On the outside, she looked as steady as a rock.

She'd never met the man who stood looking at the painting of the Vietnam Veterans Memorial in Arlington National Cemetery, but she knew who he was: Glen Moran.

She'd thought him dead, too, although in a flash she realized that news of his survival had probably made headlines in all the media. Glen was one of their own; they would have trumpeted his survival from the rooftops.

She'd just been locked so deep in her dungeon of despair that she had blocked out the news—if she had even heard it. Although Marazán had been Frank's birthplace and she had known how he felt about it, she had shied away from news programs that mentioned Marazán—when, she realized now, she shouldn't have.

Biting the inside of her bottom lip that suddenly wanted to tremble, she moved toward him, feeling as wooden as a marionette whose strings were being manipulated by a rank amateur.

"You're Glen Moran."

The last man to fly with Frank, she almost added— the man who might be able to tell her how Frank had died, what had happened, what had gone wrong with all the carefully laid plans. No one else she had contacted in those first terrible days after the accident could tell her; or *would* tell her. All she had gotten out of everyone had been the expected soothing platitudes that hadn't even touched her pain.

As if of their own accord, her hands went out to him.

"You make me wish I weren't."

Like the hands that folded around hers, his voice was gentle. Glen Moran, she sensed, was a sensitive and a compassionate, caring man.

Glen Moran would tell—would *show*—a woman that he loved her.

"Don't say that." And don't you even think what you just thought, Laura Crane, she admonished herself. Her voice was husky, a product of the dull ache that had leaped into her throat. The self-recrimination impaled her racing heart, like a bird in flight caught by a hunter's arrow.

Frank, she told herself, couldn't help the way he'd been, unable to express his innermost feelings in the words she had wanted to hear. Vietnam had done strange things to a lot of men who had survived the carnage to come home. She had no right to compare Frank with a man too young to have been there—not even when the man had seen suffering in other parts of the world; not even when the man was Glen Moran.

Compressing her lips to still a threatening tremor, she drew a breath deep into her lungs. And she had thought today was going to be so special; the day when she could look to the future, to maybe begin being happy again.

Instead, the tears she hadn't been able to shed, even at first, were back, burning behind her eyes, pooled like some fiery liquid in her throat; but no nearer to release than before.

"Frank—" the single syllable came in a choked whisper "—knew the risks of flying into Marazán and trying to land on a makeshift airstrip. You were lucky." She bit her bottom lip, which was beginning to feel tender from being nibbled at. "He wasn't."

His hands grasping hers tightened. "You're doing it again," he said quietly, giving her hands a squeeze.

"Doing what?" She barely managed to get the words past the lump in her throat.

"Making me wish I hadn't been the lucky one."

She watched the pain of his memories tramp heavy-booted across his face and could almost believe he meant it. Uncle Zeb was right: he did look as though he'd been dragged through a knothole—both emotionally and physically. The scars on his memory, she suspected, would take longer to disappear than those she could see.

She was younger than he'd expected, Glen decided as he watched her bring white mugs from a shelf behind the cash register and pour coffee from the granite pot on the potbellied stove that stood in the center of the high-ceilinged room. Her slender hand in a quilted mitt grasped the coffeepot handle in a no-nonsense manner that told him she had done it often.

Crane's Mountain, Kentucky—its general store and this woman, anyhow—were casting some kind of gentle spell over him, the same mysterious bewitchment he always felt back home at Sycamore Point.

As in Sycamore Point, he found himself thinking, a man could find himself here; find himself and what he was searching for in his life.

What sort of place—what sort of woman—had he expected to find?

In the moments before the plane crashed, Carrera had spoken of Laura Crane almost reverently, referring to her as the woman he would have liked to spend the rest of his life with. A lady with class, he had indicated by his manner if not by his words. But that, Glen reminded himself, could have been Carrera's natural, quiet reserve, his old-Spanish gallantry, speaking. The art-gallery director in Washington had called her "an artist of note," leading him to expect to find a woman nearer Frank's age, which had been fortyish—maybe forty-five or even a year or two older. Carrera had been one of those ageless men whose pursuit of danger had kept him young.

Instead, he mused now as he watched her move gracefully toward him with a mug of coffee clasped in both her hands, he would guess her to be in her middle to late twenties, a gazelle of a woman who had known sorrow but who had come through it with poise intact, perhaps more finely tuned than before. Carrera, he thought, would have been proud of her.

Taking the cup from her hands, he said "Thanks" and swore silently at the huskiness in his voice. The last thing she needed was to suspect how much the carrying of final messages to loved ones and answering their inevitable questions about last moments shook him up. He'd done it before—from Afghanistan, the Middle East, Central America, often in a language he spoke haltingly—and it was pure hell. He'd never gotten used to it.

With the merest ghost of a "You're welcome" smile, she drew a scarred captain's chair around so she could face him and sat down, her jeans-clad knees so close to his that he could lean forward and touch them. Her hands folded around the mug of steaming black coffee as it rested on her knees.

"Tell me about Frank."

Her voice was so soft it shouldn't have slashed through him with the razor sharpness of a well-honed machete, but it did.

Keenly aware of the pain, he sucked in a breath and held it. She wasn't going to make it easy—not that there was any way this conversation could be made easy. He had known that from the moment he'd given Carrera his word; and **he** had been dreading it from the moment he'd returned to consciousness in that poorly staffed, poorly equipped, poorly supplied little hospital staffed by one overworked Marazán doctor with guerrilla sympathies and a handful of young men who wore sidearms as they changed bandages.

But the instant he'd turned at the sound of that cowbell when she'd entered the store and he'd seen her, he had wanted to turn tail and run as fast as his game leg would carry him, just to keep from hurting her more than she'd already been hurt—or else take her in his arms and comfort her.

In that instant he had recognized Laura Crane as a woman he wanted to shield from pain, a woman he could come to care deeply for; like for the rest of his life. And what the hell, he wondered, was he thinking?

With an effort, he wrenched his gaze from her face, lifted the coffee mug to his lips and gulped a mouthful of the strong brew. It burned all the way down, but it was what he needed: it cleared his head.

Mentally he braced himself—as he had braced himself physically in those moments before the plane smacked into the jungle growth at the end of the landing strip; as he had braced himself many times since, in the face of excruciating pain that had seemed to be an integral part of the therapy designed to restore and strengthen shattered bone and torn flesh.

She was waiting, holding her breath, it seemed to him. He had to get on with it and stop torturing them both.

So he said, "Frank and I made a pact as the plane was going down."

No need to tell her that the first part of the pact—and he thought, sometimes, the more important part, to Carrera—had been that he finish the story he'd gone to Marazán to get. He hadn't done it yet, largely because he was in no shape physically to even attempt another entry into the revolt-torn little country.

Mariana's power trip had really taken off during the past year and a half, it appeared. Now, no foreign press was allowed inside Marazán, and the State Department seemed hamstrung, unable to do anything about it. Even the Marazán press was strictly censored, with nothing getting published about the uprising, much less sent out of the country, without the general's personal approval.

But one way or another, he vowed to himself, he would tell the story of Marazán to the world. He could still hear Carrera's quiet drawl, asking that he "tell the world of the rape of my people by their own country-men."

"Please go on." Laura's voice, breaking the silence, was soft but surprisingly steady.

He found the words he sought. "If I got out and he...didn't...he wanted me to tell you... He wanted me to tell you that you are the woman he would have liked to spend the rest of his life with."

Without speaking, she rose from the old captain's chair, walked the few feet to the counter where she placed her untouched coffee down beside a glass candy jar filled with peppermint sticks and stood there, her back to him as she looked up at the painting she'd done of the Vietnam Veterans Memorial.

Why couldn't Frank have told *her*? He'd had plenty of chances in the two years they had seen each other.

As if drawn by something beyond her control, her eyes lifted again to the Vietnam Veterans Memorial painting that—unlike her other work that filled the alcove her grandfather had fixed specially for them—hung behind the counter, where everyone who entered the store could see it.

Why, Frank? If you loved me that much, why couldn't you have said so?

She felt herself back in Arlington the day they'd met—she standing at her easel, brushing onto canvas the lean, ghostly lines of her father's face as she remembered him before he'd returned to the active duty that would take him to Vietnam when he volunteered for the tour....

"Lady, you're good."

Frank's easy drawl echoed in her memory. She'd brushed in the jawline of the superimposed face against the sky—the square jaw that had always made her father look like an officer who had seen hard duty even when he was digging bait to go fishing down on the lake—before she looked over her shoulder into intense black eyes that had seemed to reach for her soul.

Grateful for the approval, she had thanked him. Her previous work had been mostly nature studies, of birds and animals in her native Cumberland Mountains, for which the art world was just beginning to recognize her. In fact, her reason for being in Washington then was a one-woman show in a prestigious gallery.

"It's my private Vietnam memorial. My father died there."

"A lot of good men did. A lot more...left the best part of themselves there."

Frank had stuck his hands deeper into pockets of baggy camouflage trousers that, she had thought, looked as if they'd also survived Vietnam although they had probably come from some war-surplus store, and leaned over her shoulder to get a closer look at the painting.

In her mind's eye, Laura saw her hand touch the paintbrush to the glob of pale gray, the ghostly, luminescent gray that she had mixed on her palette, and saw the brush touching canvas as clearly as though she had time-traveled into the past....

"Are you all right?"

The sound of Glen's voice, so gentle and caring that she felt a sudden, inexplicable urge to turn into his arms and stay there forever, brought her back.

Chapter Two

When she didn't respond, Glen silently cursed the stupid question.

How *could* she be all right? A part of her had died in that Marazán jungle, and after nearly eighteen months—months that she'd undoubtedly spent trying to put her life back together—he had popped out of the blue to dredge up all the shock and sorrow.

If she had loved Frank Carrera as deeply as, Glen was sure, Carrera had loved her, she might never be whole again; might never love as deeply—or let another man love her. It would be a pity.

"Yes," she whispered, finally answering him, but still not moving as she stood looking up at the painting.

Except for the single husky syllable that sounded as if it had been wrenched from the depths of her soul, she might have been a figure transfixed in front of an altar—an altar that was the painting of the Vietnam Veterans Memorial bearing her distinctive signature of a crane in flight across her name scrawled in a corner.

Watching, he wondered what significance the painting held for her, other than being one of her own.

The face that seemed to be watching from the heavens wasn't Carrera's but was that of a man older than most 'Nam soldiers. Carrera had told him once that he'd completed two tours of duty, most of the time piloting an evacuation helicopter between the front lines and hospitals, and had been twenty-six when the war ended.

Even more faintly, she murmured, "No. No, I'm not all right." She took a deep breath. "But I will be."

She sounded determined to make it so.

At the door, the tall black dog that had whimpered to be let in now howled its frustration and began to scratch agitatedly at the screen.

Laura seemed not to hear.

Taking his gaze off her rigid back, Glen reached down to set his coffee mug on the floor, then pushed himself up out of the chair, wincing at the pain brought on by the stretching of back, shoulder and thigh muscles. Almost any movement still brought pain, although he sometimes thought it was growing less excruciating as time passed.

The dog whined again, then seemed to wait understandingly as Glen walked stiffly to the door, trying not to favor his bad leg. He had no idea whether the dog was allowed inside the store or not, but it sure wanted in and it looked heavy enough and rangy enough to back up, take aim at the old-looking screen wire and come right through.

And after a year of virtually learning to walk again, Glen sympathized with anything that dove through *anything*—although the dive he had taken through the plane's shattered cockpit glass had only been the beginning of his troubles, and had been far from the worst of them.

Determined not to think about that now, he tried to close his mind to the rest of it.

"This may be getting us both in trouble, fella," he muttered as he opened the door for the dog to enter the store.

As it had when he'd come through, the cowbell over the door jangled. Also as before, no one appeared to see who had come into the store. Glen was beginning to think the coffee had made itself.

Ignoring him, the dog trotted straight to Laura's side, where it sat on its haunches and gazed adoringly up at her. As Glen watched, she seemed to come out of her trance. One of her hands dropped to the dog's broad, shaggy crown.

Glen let go the breath that had stopped in his lungs, as his breathing had a tendency to do whenever he looked at her. Did he only imagine some of the tension had gone from her?

Some of his own tension relaxed, as well, allowing him to hate himself less for having hurt her by reminding her of her loss. No matter how important it was, in his mind, for her to know that Carrera's last thought had been of her, he wished someone else had delivered the message. She would never be able to look at him without remembering the anguish he had caused her.

"You let Brewster in," she said huskily, turning at last to face him. "Thank you."

She sounded so vulnerable that he wanted to reach out for her.

"You looked like you could use a friend."

Bracing himself to hide his pain from her, he walked back across the store—a large, rectangular room—that appeared to be Crane General Mercantile's "Groc., Hdwe., & Sundries," all rolled into one.

"Besides," he continued, all but gritting his teeth against the grinding pain that rolled through him, "dang dog was about to come through the screen to reach you."

She seemed to find the smile that lifted the corners of her mouth easily enough but to have trouble keeping it on her lips. He couldn't miss the angst that flashed over her face.

"Sometimes I think Brewster has a canine sixth sense where I'm concerned. He knows when I'm hurting. Don't you, friend?"

With the words, she buried her face in the dog's shaggy black ruff.

When she lifted her head, Glen had a fresh cup of coffee poured and ready to hand to her.

She took it smilingly.

"I'm beginning to think Brewster isn't the only one who has a sixth sense where I'm concerned." She resurrected the smile. "I needed this. Thank you."

"I caused you pain. The least I can do is offer you caffeine."

Fearing she would read the truth behind his words—
that he wanted to offer her a lot more than a cup of
coffee—Glen turned from her to refill his own cup.

The stove stood virtually in the center of the store.
As he poured his coffee, he tried to imagine the place
in winter, with the stove glowing red, chairs drawn up
close around it and men like the old codger who still
dozed on the front porch swapping tales while snow
fell thickly and wind howled down the mountain and
through the valleys.

He failed. The only face he could picture was Laura's, haunted by her grief.

Fleeing the poignant sensations the vision aroused,
he lifted the cup to his lips and tasted the brew; it was
stronger than the first cup had been. Taking a hefty
swallow, he focused on the windowed alcove across the
store. He'd noticed it as he came in, but had been
drawn like a hummingbird to nectar by the painting of
the Vietnam Veterans Memorial on the back wall.

Grasping his mug of coffee in both hands, he
walked around the stove and two straight-backed
chairs drawn up across from each other at a checkerboard. The checkerboard, checkers in place on the red
and black squares, appeared to be balanced rather
precariously on a nail keg.

With his awkward gait, Glen skirted a glass-fronted,
glass-topped counter that displayed colorful tied flies,
gaudy live-rubber wriggly worms and assorted other
fishing paraphernalia. A small sign inside the case
read: Live Bait On Order.

On top of the counter stood a larger, hand-lettered
sign adorned with a speckled trout leaping, lifelike,

from sparkling water. "Laura Crane" was written all over it although it was unsigned.

Cabins On Lake
By Week-End, Week Or Month

Tempted, he told himself *no*. He had delivered Carrera's message, as he'd promised to do. Now be smart, he told himself somewhat sternly. Answer her questions and get the heck out, away from reminders of what happened, back to D.C. Finish the writing job you began at Sycamore Point.

And what then? he wondered. John Baz, his editor, had told him a desk job was his any time he wanted it.

A desk job? The prospect scared the hell out of him. He'd be bored out of his skull in a month, going out a ninth-floor window in two.

The alcove had been built of rustic planks—red cedar, he knew from the warm glow and peeling gray rusty-brownish bark and the aromatic scent that filled his nostrils—a part of the old store but apart from it.

The outside wall was all of glass—small, rectangular panes reminiscent of another era—that presented a vista of green mountains and a blue sky boiling with cumuli. A clear north light spilled into the alcove onto the matted and framed pictures that hung on the two walls that extended into the store.

There was no fourth wall, which made the little gallery indisputably a part of Crane's General Mercantile.

Pausing, Glen drew a breath of the cedary fragrance deep into his lungs. The outdoorsy scent, and the natural setting provided by the cedar walls and the many windows, were perfect for the small show. The birds and small animals that were the subjects of the prints, oils and watercolors seemed totally at home in their depicted habitats, and so lifelike, they appeared ready to break for cover if he got too close.

When Laura touched his arm he jumped, then swore silently at himself for allowing the edginess that was still with him, hovering on the verge of consciousness, to intrude on the moment.

"You're stalling."

Her voice was low, faintly accusing.

Feeling as though the honeybees had zoomed out of the sketch on the wall and zeroed in on him, he folded a hand over hers, on his arm.

She would have been better off if she had let him go on stalling, Laura thought when she had heard his account of the flight that had been Frank's last; and of Frank's final moments as Glen had known them.

Frank's last thoughts being of her had touched her deeply, the way Glen related them....

They had taken off from Miami, Glen told her, and had flown across the Gulf, the shortest distance to Marazán from the point where the relief supplies had been collected. Glen described it as a "beautiful flight."

If he'd felt any apprehension, it had been about what awaited him when he struck off through the countryside toward Marazán City, the capital; about the obstacles he might find thrown up there to thwart his investigation of the corruption his old newspaper acquaintance, Juan Hernández, had told him about—the story, he told her, that Frank had wanted him to write.

The prospect of landing on a runway hacked out of the jungle hadn't worried him especially. He had, he told her, taken bigger chances with pilots less skilled than he had known Carrera to be.

Frank, he also said, had planned to visit the mission, where he had friends, while the Spanish-blooded Indians, the *mestizos*, unloaded the aircraft. Then Frank had planned to take off immediately, to spend Christmas with her.

The "friends" Frank had intended to visit were the same people she had tried to talk to after his death. The people she had begged to tell her what had happened to him and whose fear had been palpable even over the phone.

Why hadn't they told her that Glen Moran had survived the crash?

"It's doubtful they knew," Glen replied when she put the question into words. "From what I was told—much later, when I finally came around—no one outside that miserable little hut in the jungle knew I was alive. And they were scared to death someone would find out. It was a matter of life and death—*theirs*."

She drew in a deep breath. "So what happens now?"

"What d'you mean?"

Lifting her eyes to meet his intense gaze, she asked, "Are you going back?"

It was a question she had no right to ask, she realized. He'd very nearly died in the Marazán jungle—he had been in hospitals for over a year and he still wore his pain like a second skin she knew he wished was invisible. He had given her a graphic description of how it had been, for him and for Frank. Elements in power in Marazán—and some among those who rebelled against the use of power and were just as dishonest— didn't want him or any other journalist, native or foreign, exposing their corruption.

She had no right to suggest, even with a question mark at the end of the sentence, that he place himself in that kind of jeopardy again.

He answered her, finally. "As soon as I can move like I'm younger than a hundred and seven."

"And how long will that be?" she asked, smiling in spite of the heaviness that had again settled in her chest.

"Three or four, maybe five months." He seemed unsure. "The doctors say exercise and time. 'Let nature take its course' is the best medicine now. Thank God. I've had my share of orthopedic ropes and pulleys and therapy."

Laura combed her fingers through Brewster's shaggy ruff. The dog responded by rolling brown eyes at her and lolling its pink tongue out. The expression on its jet face was pure pleasure.

Ropes and pulleys and therapy, to say nothing of the struggle to stay alive that had preceded the orthopedic sessions, sounded pretty grim to her.

Her own therapy, self-prescribed, had involved walks in the mountains she'd grown up in and loved, often with Brewster tagging along at her heels. Other times, she had huddled, hunched against the chill that sometimes had cut to her bones, as she'd watched the creatures of nature cope with their environment that often was harsh, even in the generally mild Cumberlands. Long sessions with a sketch pad or at her easel had comforted her.

Forcing herself to go back into other people's worlds, face the truth, field well-meant words of sympathy, had been the hardest.

No, she reflected. Not thinking of what might have been, not thinking of what she had lost, not letting herself feel sorry for herself, had been the most difficult. More than once, she'd lost those battles and had fallen into the bottomless crevasses of self-pity.

But as soon as he was able, Glen Moran had come looking for her—a stranger, for no reason other than that he had given his word. For no reason, she realized, than that he'd cared and wanted her to know Frank had died thinking of her. It touched her heart.

For the first time in his life, Glen thought, he envied a dog. And that big black devil— What was he, anyhow? Part Newfoundland, part Irish Wolfhound? He grinned to himself. Part black bear? Brewster seemed to accept her attention as his due. Resting his broad muzzle on her knees and closing his eyes, the dog seemed to bask in her presence.

Glen felt the inner smile lift the corners of his mouth. They made quite a picture, those two: the big black dog that looked capable of taking on a grizzly; and Laura, maybe five-feet-eight, willowy, with that mass of shining chestnut hair tumbling around her face as she bent over the animal, murmuring to it.

As though he understood her whispered words, Brewster lifted his head off her knees, stretched his large frame, then rose languidly and sauntered into the alcove where he flopped on the woven rug in front of the window as though he'd done it before. He looked, Glen decided, more like a bear than a dog.

Grinning, he said, "Some dog."

"Yes, he is. I've had him since he was a puppy." She laughed softly, a lilting sound that lifted Glen's spirits. "Would you believe the runt of the litter?" she asked as her gaze went to Brewster, who again was at peace with his world.

"I'd like to see the others."

She smiled. "I can show them to you; they're four years old now and all of them are within a couple of miles of here as a crow flies. I did a sketch of all of them together when they were three weeks old. It's over my fireplace."

"I'll settle for that," Glen said, grinning at her again. He wondered where her fireplace was located.

"All right. Any time you say, but you're going to have to walk." The warning was light-toned. "This is rough and rugged country."

Her smile broadened, tantalizingly slowly. "Your car is as close to where I live as it can get. Not even my four-wheel-drive can make it up the trail. I park out behind the store and backpack everything up. The trail's pretty steep in spots."

Sadness seemed to settle in on her face, giving it a look of vulnerability that squeezed Glen's heart.

"Frank called the house my aerie, although it's not a stronghold at all—more like a fairy-tale house of cedar and pine and oak, with lots of windows that invite my mountains inside."

Glen smiled at her choice of words. "Then the woman at the gallery in D.C. was right. She said Crane's Mountain means more to you than a mailing address."

"A lot more," Laura admitted huskily. Nodding, she gave him a searching look. "Is that how you found me? The gallery?"

"Partly. Actually, Carrera's sister in Brownsville, Carmelita, pointed me in the right direction." It had taken time to find Carmelita, too. Carrera sure hadn't been free with information about his private life. "She had a sketch of an eagle in flight that she had found among his things. It had the gallery stamp on the back."

He thought her self-control was going to dissolve in the tears that suddenly glistened in her eyes. Her hands were clasped tightly in her lap, her lips pressed tight. But she didn't cry. And when she spoke, her voice was steady.

"Frank went straight to the gallery from Arlington after watching me finish Daddy's face in the 'Nam painting—" her glance strayed to the picture, clung for a moment, then came back to his "—and bought the eagle. It was his favorite, he said, of all the things in my show."

"Carrera was something of an eagle in flight himself," Glen said softly, feeling a pang of grief for his friend, and meaning every word. "Maybe he felt he'd found a kindred spirit—'' in both her and the flying eagle she had sketched.

Unable to stop himself, he reached for her hands, folding them inside his own.

Laura sold two peppermint sticks to Joanie Lewellyn, who eyed Glen with open curiosity while Laura's grandfather—who had returned from someplace out behind the store—explained to another customer in his booming voice which fly was best for speckled trout and which for bass. Laura doubted the greenhorn knew a trout from a minnow.

When she waved as the little girl danced out the door, she saw that Glen was back in the alcove, apparently lost in the other wall of her sketches, oils and watercolors. The intensity with which he studied them made her smile.

As she watched, he moved from a pen-and-ink drawing of a striped skunk and her kits to a river scene in which a barefoot youth with overalls rolled to his knees fished off a boulder in the middle of a stretch of white water. Glen's movement from in front of one picture to in front of another, accomplished with a definite limp, caused pain to skitter across his face— and her heart to go out to him.

How she wanted to help him.

Not so that he could go back to Marazán and get himself shot at again, but, she told herself, because he had been Frank's friend; because he had cared enough to come looking for her, just so he could tell her Frank had died loving her; because Frank had asked him to find her.

If he hadn't come, she mused, who but he would have known? And even if someone else had known, could that person have blamed Glen for getting on with his own life first? He had lost such a chunk of his life—the same nearly eighteen months that were gone from hers, she realized with a flash of empathy.

What had he said the doctors had told him? Exercise, and time; let nature take its course....

Well, what better place for nature to take its course than right here on Crane's Mountain? The Cumberlands were great for healing fractured spirits. Witness her own. Mightn't those same healing powers extend to broken bodies, as well?

The speculation surprised her.

Lord love her, she'd just thought how great it could be to have Glen at the lake for the summer!

Chapter Three

The kid fishing off the rock in the painting reminded Glen of himself at that age: thirteen, maybe fourteen, using a cane pole and a hook baited with worms he'd dug or crickets he'd caught.

There'd been no white water like the rushing mountain stream Laura had painted, though. The Wabash, back home at Sycamore Point, was a gentle stream except when it flooded, usually in the spring when he had been in school and daydreaming of the long, lazy days of summer that waited for him to fill them with the things boys usually did.

Looking at the painting, he felt a little like Huck Finn grown up; or rather, as he imagined a grown-up Huck Finn would have felt if Mark Twain had gotten around to writing another book about the character. He felt a little nostalgic, homesick for the simple life

he had left behind years ago, when he'd left Sycamore Point for the first time.

If only he could wipe out all those years between
that time and now.... No, he didn't mean that, he told
himself. Good things had happened to him during
those years. He had grown professionally, realized at
least some of his dreams, been recognized for his
work. He had gone home to Sycamore Point for a
blissful time—even though that blissful time had been
part of a Drug Enforcement Administration sting op-
eration that had sent him undercover again.

He had also come close to buying that big newspaper in the sky, down in Marazán. What had happened
had given him pause, made him stop and take a long,
hard look at his life. And it had led to his decision that
his life definitely needed restructuring.

The months of recuperation he'd just spent at Sycamore Point after getting out of all those hospitals
had begun to renew more than just his body. He knew,
now, what he wanted out of life—and it wasn't another Pulitzer that John Baz assured him would be his
when he wrapped up the Marazán story.

Let somebody else take the bows, pick up the prizes,
get slapped on the back at the Washington Press Club.
All he wanted was a place to settle down—maybe Sycamore Point or just a gentle place like it where the
living was good—and write; a woman to share it with,
a family...

What the hell was he thinking? he asked himself.
Chasing hard news had been his life—*was* his life.
Until this last stay at Sycamore Point, the search for
the warmth and serenity, the mask of a country boy

come home to pasture, had been a carefully planned part of the facade.

Remembering, Glen grunted. He'd been hoisted on his own petard, he told himself. And he knew it wasn't true. The longing had always been there, buried under the ambition: the enjoyment of hot pursuit of a story.

Suddenly conscious of Laura's approach, he turned to her with what he hoped was a reminiscent smile, the kind of smile her painting of the boy fishing would inspire.

"Takes me back," he said, nodding at the painting.

Without hesitation, she stepped forward, lifted the picture off the wall and held it out to him.

"It's yours."

He started to say he couldn't accept it, or at least wanted to pay for it, but found himself unable to utter the words. He had hurt her enough without refusing a gift that expressed her gratitude with gracious candor.

Not understanding the emotion that rushed through him, he said "Thank you" a trifle hoarsely, as his hands covered hers on the wooden picture frame.

"You're welcome."

Her blue eyes meeting his were eloquent with an expression he wished she had put into words.

He couldn't *not* smile. "I'll hang it over my fireplace—when I get a fireplace again."

There was a fireplace—more than one, actually—at his old homeplace in Sycamore Point. But Laini, D.J. and Murphy lived there now. He'd just spent the few months he'd been out of the hospital with them. His apartment in D.C., where he was headed now, had always been a place to hang his hat when he was between overseas assignments—most of them in places like Marazán, he reflected ruefully.

Sometimes he wondered why he was going back to his apartment in Washington. Lord knew the house at Sycamore Point was large enough for him to have gone on living there, working on his book, flying to D.C. for checkups and the occasional periods of intensive therapy that he still needed.

But in Sycamore Point he'd also have been envying D.J. and Laini the happiness they had found together; watching Murphy grow, and wishing he hadn't focused quite so much on his career through all the years he couldn't live over again.

Laura's smile was bright, and warm, and as natural on her full lips as the sunlight on the mountain he could see through the alcove windows.

"One fireplace coming up," she announced lightly.

Why the hell did he feel as if his hands had fused to hers? She had given him a painting that said thanks for having been Carrera's friend . . . for coming to tell her about the man she loved.

That was all.

He would do well, he cautioned himself, to remember that.

"How's that?" The words seemed to rise from some bewitching mist that filled his need in spite of self-admonition against letting it take possession of his senses.

"Grandpa has a few cabins down on the lake. There's a fireplace in each one."

Lifting his gaze from the painting—and her hands, which felt as if they belonged in his—to her face, Glen managed to say with a grin, "And tourists lined up three deep to rent each one, no doubt."

"Business isn't that good. There's always a cabin or two vacant."

Was that *invitation* rather than gratitude he read in her eyes? He wanted to believe—oh, he wanted to believe that it was.

"We'd love to have you as our guest," she continued.

Disengaging her hands from his—and leaving him acutely conscious of the warmth of her touch that lingered on the smoothly sanded wood frame—she said, "The Cumberlands in summer can work wonders for a wounded body and psyche." She paused. "You should give it a try."

"Believe me, I'm tempted." By more than the mountains working "wonders" for his body and spirit, Glen wanted to tell her. And wondered what her reaction would be if he did.

"I might even loan you Brewster to walk with you. If you get lost, he could guide you home."

"My cabin or your house?"

The words, uttered in a teasing voice, came as naturally as though he'd known her a lot longer than a couple of hours. He'd met her under circumstances that would make him a first-class bastard if he took advantage of her vulnerability.

"The store." She grinned. "It's where he always brings lost greenhorns."

"Touché," Glen said, grinning back at her, glad to see she wasn't going to treat him as though he were fragile.

Leaning forward, with the picture between them, he kissed her on the forehead. "Thanks for the painting."

Laura Crane, he decided, could take care of herself emotionally. He'd best learn in a hurry to do the same where his feelings for her were concerned.

"Did I hear my granddaughter call you a greenhorn a few moments ago, Mr. Moran?"

Laura smiled at both men as her grandfather—finally rid of the customer who apparently had wanted to learn all there was to know about fishing in one easy lesson—stuck out a gnarled hand.

Holding on to the painting with his other hand, Glen grasped it.

"'Fraid so, sir." Glen's glance sought hers. "She's probably right. I haven't been in the Cumberlands before. From what I've seen, it's beautiful country."

"It is that. Can't be beat for hunting, fishing or just plain sitting in the shade and relaxing. Got some great hiking trails, too."

Her grandfather's pride in the mountains they both loved echoed in his voice, but, Laura mused, he also sounded like the chamber of commerce. What could Crane's Mountain, Kentucky, offer a man like Glen Moran, who lived on excitement? The town, if it could be called that, wouldn't be on the map except for the "post-office corner" that until recently—before the

USPS "streamlined" service to remote rural areas, a move that had eliminated numerous small post offices—had been behind the store's cash register.

Moving cautiously, Glen leaned the painting against the alcove wall.

Pretending not to watch his every move, Laura managed not to wince visibly as he slowly straightened to his six-feet-two- or three-inch height. Pain, she suspected, gnawed at him constantly and he seemed to make a valiant effort to live with it.

"Sounds like what the doctor ordered," Glen answered, as his glance flickered to her face, where it lingered for a moment and warmed the cockles of her heart. "Laura told me you have cabins. I'd like to rent one—probably for the summer, though I can't say for sure right now how long I'll be here."

Laura opened her mouth to say, "I thought you said..." or, "I invited you to be our guest, remember?" No sound came.

As though he had read her mind, Glen grinned. "I know what I said: I was tempted. Let's just say I gave in to temptation."

The sparks that danced in his brown eyes struck a responsive fire in her.

"I don't know what's going on here—" her grandfather sounded genuinely baffled but amused and pleased "—but welcome to Crane's Mountain, Mr. Moran."

"Glen," Glen corrected.

And Laura decided *she* didn't know what was happening, either—to *her*. She felt closer to happiness than she had for a long time.

It didn't make sense. No way could the sharp burst of pleasure that made her feel almost lightheaded have anything to do with Glen Moran. How could it? she asked herself, when he had stirred up all the misery and grief she'd thought earlier that morning she had put behind her?

An hour later, down at the cabin Glen had rented, Laura stepped back from the fireplace over which she had hung the painting of the boy fishing with as much care as if she'd been hanging it for one of her one-woman shows around the country.

"There!" Her glance sought Glen's. "How's that?"

"Couldn't have done it better myself." A smile tugged at the corners of his wide mouth as he surveyed the result of her handiwork. "Or enjoyed it as much."

The same warmth that had rushed through her blood vessels when she'd sensed his eyes on her as she stretched to hang the picture just so, swept over her again. Fleeing the sensation, she glanced back at the painting.

"Anything worth doing is worth doing right."

"My sentiment exactly."

Walking over, he took the tack hammer she had left on the mantel after hanging the painting and pressed it into her hand, carefully folding her fingers over its smooth wooden handle. The hammer was from her grandfather's toolbox.

"Thanks for helping me move in." He spoke softly, with his hands still cradling hers.

Laura felt as though her senses were centered in the hand he held in his. In that moment, she felt something was happening between them. And she wasn't sure she was ready for it. She *knew* she didn't understand it.

Summoning a smile, she gently disengaged her hand from his clasp. ''Part of the service, sir.''

With those lightly spoken words, she glanced around the cabin's combination living room-kitchen. Off the larger room was a bedroom with two bunk beds. She had brought down everything she could think of that he might need, and even stocked the fridge. He had insisted on paying for the food.

''If you need anything else,'' she said, completing a mental checklist, ''holler.''

''Since I plan to eat the fish I catch on that cane pole your grandfather so optimistically gave me,'' he responded, grinning, ''that's not likely.'' Even as a kid he hadn't been the world's greatest fisherman, being given to throwing back more than he kept—catching more dreams than fish.

''Good luck.''

Smiling, she edged toward the door that opened onto the deck. Brewster, who had loped along after Glen's car the short distance from the store, lifted his head off huge forepaws and thumped his tail on the deck planking, plainly asking what had taken her so long.

''And feel free,'' she continued, ''to use the phone at the store.''

Glen Moran, she mused, would probably get phone calls, and make some. Among the luggage she had helped him bring in from the car had been a personal computer and a modem he had told her helped him tap into research sources. He hoped, he'd said, to get some work done on a book.

"There won't be many calls."

Using the cane now, he followed her to the door. "Drive the car back if you like. I won't be using it."

"Oh, but you—"

"I'm here for Crane's Cumberland Mountain Magic Therapy, highly recommended for what ails me," Glen reminded her with a smile.

Laura couldn't help smiling back. But she didn't take the car. He *might* need it.

Besides, she thought as she struck off along the road around the lake, Brewster at her side, she needed a good dose of "Crane's Cumberland Mountain Magic Therapy" herself—for reasons totally different from his . . . far different from the recuperation of her soul she'd needed it for previously.

"Come on, Brewster," she called to the dog when he lagged behind to nose around a chunk of rock that jutted out of the thin, rocky soil along the lakeshore. "Let's run."

Sometimes it helped.

Laura herself was Crane's Cumberland Mountain Magic Therapy personified—for him, anyway, Glen thought as he watched her break into a run, her bright chestnut hair bouncing on her shoulders.

She ran seemingly effortlessly, a picture of grace and beauty that stirred his senses, heated his blood, caused his heart to beat faster. He needed a cold shower, or a dip in that sunlit lake.

How long had it been since he'd had such an instant response to a woman he'd barely met? Good God, he was acting like a high-school freshman with a crush on a sexy senior cheerleader who wouldn't give him the time of day, not like a mature thirty-seven-year-old man who should know better.

Leaning against the doorjamb, with the weight off his bad leg, he watched until Laura vanished around a jog in the road. Then, using the cane, he walked carefully across the deck and down the steps, holding on to the banister, in case his leg gave way, as it sometimes did, though it happened less frequently now.

After driving the Buick up close alongside the cabin where it wouldn't interfere with his view of the lake and the mountains, he went back inside. Tossing his keys onto the mantel, he stood looking at the painting, imagining himself perched on that boulder, getting his feet and his seat wet even if he didn't appear to be catching any fish.

Laura Crane was a good artist, he mused, as was obvious not just in this picture but in the others he'd seen, the wildlife ones.

As he'd stood in front of that painting of the 'Nam memorial, he had choked up, just as he did every time he tried to walk the length of that black marble monument in Arlington. Every time, he felt as though he were kin to each man whose name was there.

And he hadn't even been in 'Nam.

Laura's painting had made him feel the jumbled emotions all over again.

"Hey."

"Hey."

Glen turned.

"Hey, yourselves," he said, greeting the two youngsters. He recognized the girl; she had been in the store. The boy—who looked so much like her they had to be brother and sister—might be five, which would make him maybe two years younger than the girl.

"Can we come in, mister?"

"Yeah, can we?"

"Why don't I come out?" Glen asked, and, without waiting for an answer, walked toward the door, conscious of their fascination with his cane. "We can sit in the sun and watch the boats on the lake."

He had seen two boats a while ago—a skiff with a bright yellow triangular sail and a single occupant who appeared at the distance to be a teenage girl, and an outboard with two fishermen aboard. The outboard's motor had been throttled back to trolling speed, and both men had been lolling back, taking it easy while their hooks and lines dragged through the water behind the boat.

Pushing open the door, he went out onto the deck. The outboard had disappeared around the point, leaving only the small sailboat hovering on the water like a yellow-winged white bird. Its bikini-clad occupant relaxed at the tiller.

"That's our mom," the girl announced, pointing toward the sailboat.

Cautiously Glen seated himself on the top step, trying to ignore the dull ache in his thigh muscles where the bullet had torn through.

"She's a pretty good sailor," he commented, feeling that they expected him to say something. To him, anyone was a "good sailor" who didn't end up capsizing the boat.

"She's pretty," the girl said.

"Yeah. Beautiful," the boy chimed in, without taking his eyes off Glen's cane leaning against his leg, and Glen's hand as it worked at the cramping muscles.

She also had a cheering section, Glen thought. Flexing his thigh muscles, he hoped the children were just passing by, on their way to meet their mother at the boat dock around the lake.

Kids got to him real easy, he admitted to himself. Witness Murphy, he reflected with a rush of homesickness for the boy.

"How'd you get hurt?" the boy asked. His hazel eyes grew wide and round as they focused on Glen's hands massaging his thigh muscles through his jeans.

Thinking, Oh, hell, Glen replied, "I had an accident."

The massage wasn't working; his upper leg, its muscles in spasm now, felt as hard as a board. He needed to walk, and it wouldn't be a pretty sight for two young children to see: him lurching along like a drunk until his muscles loosened up enough to support his weight on an even keel.

"In a car?" The boy's eyes filled with sudden tears. "Our daddy was killed in a car wreck."

Glen stopped rubbing his thigh and touched the child's shoulder. "Sorry to hear that, buddy."

"His name's Eddie—" the girl corrected him seriously, as though she thought Glen should have known "—after our daddy."

"And what's yours?" Glen asked, glad of a chance to change the subject.

"Joanie. 'Cause that's our mom's name, and our daddy named me after her."

"Nice name."

"Was it a car wreck that hurt you?" the boy persisted.

Glen reached over and tousled the boy's sunbleached hair.

"No, Eddie. An airplane."

The hazel eyes widened. "You crashed?"

"Yep," Glen said, and realized that for better or for worse, he had become an instant hero in the boy's eyes.

It made him uncomfortable—more uncomfortable than did the thought of limping like a hamstrung horse while the kids stared. Hell, he didn't feel like a hero.

Reaching for his cane, which he had placed on the deck behind him, and grasping the banister with the other hand, he pushed and pulled himself awkwardly to his feet.

"Where's Brewster?" Eddie Lewellyn shouted the moment he entered the store ahead of his mother and sister, late that afternoon, and saw Laura behind the counter.

When Laura was in the store—which she was today because her grandfather had driven "Uncle" Zeb to his appointment with a doctor at the clinic over in Lanier—Brewster was usually available for a romp.

"Off chasing varmints, most likely," Laura answered. "He found a hot scent down by the lake this morning. Maybe he went back down there."

Eddie whirled on one bare heel.

"Whoa, buster! Not so fast!" Jo Lewellyn blocked the doorway before her young son could dart through it. "We're picking up the groceries your grandmother ordered and then we're going home to cook out—remember?"

Glancing at Laura, she grimaced. "Wienies again. I'm so sick of hot dogs on sticks I could scream, but Mom and Dad Lewellyn say if that's what the kids want, that's what they get, at least while they're here."

"But, Mom—"

"But, Mom—" Joanie echoed her brother's plaintive protest. Laura wasn't sure whether it was about the hot dogs or going off to find Brewster.

"No," their mother said in a no-nonsense tone that made Laura want to smile. Jo Lewellyn wasn't fooling anyone, especially her children, Laura suspected. Jo had a marshmallow heart where her kids were concerned. "It's getting close to dusk, and I'm sure Brewster has plans of his own for the evening.

"Brewster," Jo continued, her attention coming back to Laura, "probably isn't the only one with plans for tonight. At least I hope he isn't."

Ignoring her friend's invitation to tell all, Laura wondered what Joanie had told her mother about seeing Glen in the store that morning. Joanie had been all eyes and ears, and she was a precocious youngster.

It would have been something romantic, no doubt. That thought warmed her inside.

"All right." Jo's shrug was an exaggeration in eloquence. "Pretend he isn't tall, dark and doesn't have a mysterious scar and a limp he got when he crashed his airplane."

Had Glen gone for a walk already and encountered the children, or had they ferreted him out all by themselves?

Taking a deep breath, Laura explained that Glen had been Frank's copilot on the Marazán flight. "He's been out of the hospital only a few months and he has taken one of the cabins for the summer, until he gets his strength back."

Jo gave her a look packed with wisdom.

"Just don't go falling in love with him out of pity or empathy or whatever you want to call it. Me," she announced in that no-nonsense voice Laura realized hid a lot of anguish, even after a year, "I've decided the next man in my life—if there ever is another one—will be a dull, nonadventurous type who never drives or rides in anything that goes faster than fifty-five miles an hour."

Her husband had died a year ago in a stock-car race in Georgia; Jo had been devastated.

"Grab a bag, kids—" Jo scooped up the largest and heaviest of the brown paper sacks on the counter "—and let's get home before Grandma decides I've taken you back to the city."

Jo took a deep breath. "Don't I wish," she added in a whisper to Laura, who was handing grocery bags down into waiting young hands.

"You know you don't mean that," Laura murmured back.

Sighing, Jo said, "I know I don't. Spending summers here is important to the kids. They love the farm. And I do want them to grow up close to Eddie's folks." She exhaled audibly and added, "But I miss them so much I can hardly wait for weekends."

Laura smiled. "I know you do."

Hefting the bag, which bulged with supplies the Lewellyns didn't grow in their garden, she cautioned, "Don't forget what I said about nice, dull, nonadventurous men. They may not be as exciting as the swashbuckling charmers, but they're usually around longer."

"I'll remember that," Laura promised with a smile that was deckled with her own pain.

Hurrying to the door, she held the screen open so the cowbell wouldn't lose its clapper jangling through three hurried exits.

"Hey!" Eddie cried gleefully, almost dropping his sack of cereals as Brewster bounded up the porch steps to greet him. "Brewster!"

"Hey!" Joanie echoed excitedly. "It's Glen!"

"Joanie," her mother began, only to have the little girl interrupt.

"It's all right, Mom. He said we could call him Glen."

Laura's heart lurched into a faster beat. Everything Jo had said between "nice" and "exciting" promptly exited her mind.

Glen was both—and so much more, it frightened her.

Chapter Four

"Great kids," Glen remarked, waving back at Eddie and Joanie as they hung out the windows of the small car. Their mother eased the vehicle through gear changes and drove away from the general mercantile store at a sedate pace.

So sedate a clip, Laura mused, that the sharp little sports car must be chomping at the bit. Eddie, Sr., who had bought the car for Jo on their eighth wedding anniversary only a few months before his death, would have been out of there like a bat, tires squealing, peeling rubber, spinning gravel. And his kids would have loved it.

Also waving to the children, Laura glanced up, into a smile that jolted her senses. A breath hung up in her throat. Lord love her, couldn't she even look at Glen Moran without feeling as though she had stuck her finger in a light socket?

"They gave me quite a welcome earlier." Glen stopped waving and shoved his hand into a pocket of his jeans. "As well as the family history. Including a few things I'm sure their mother would rather they hadn't told a stranger."

Trying to corral her stampeded senses, Laura smiled back. "I can imagine." She felt her smile broaden of its own accord. "If you don't like kids, you may have yourself a problem."

"How's that?"

"Well—" she hesitated "—it's evident they like you, and when Eddie and Joanie like someone, they tend to let it all hang out."

Was that sound way down deep in Glen's throat a strangled groan? Then she thought, he *doesn't* like kids. And she did.

Her heart sinking, she sternly reminded herself that *that* was neither here nor there. Glen wasn't the man for her—he wouldn't be, even if, or when, she could put the past behind her. She would be a fool to love another man who put his wild dreams—and wild goose chases to pursue them—ahead of her!

In her grandfather's absence, she had things to do before locking up for the night, and she had better concentrate on doing them, she reminded herself. She would think about Glen later: when there was distance between them, when she was safely in her little house up the mountain, and Glen and his charisma that she couldn't seem to ignore were in his cabin down on the lake.

Maybe then, she mused, she could think straight.

You're not about to fall in love with a man you've barely met, she warned herself—no matter how attracted you are to him.

You did that once. And look at the heartbreak it brought! Glen—somehow she managed not to look at him—was like Frank: too caring about people trapped in the woes of the world for his own good.

With a sigh, she told herself that some woman would break her heart over Glen Moran. But it wouldn't be her.

Steeling herself, she led the way toward the steps that led up to the porch at the front of the store. If she was smart, she reiterated the self-warning, it wouldn't be Laura Crane.

As they climbed the steps, Laura pretended not to notice that Glen's limp seemed worse than it had appeared that morning, when—sometimes—he hadn't used the cane. Now he seemed to lean heavily on it.

His jaw appeared clenched. The jagged scar shone livid against a tan that his months at Sycamore Point had restored after all that time spent in hospital beds. His knuckles were white in the light from the bulb over the door as he grasped the head of his cane with one hand and the banister with the other. Getting himself up the steps seemed to be a major effort. It was all she could do not to put out a hand to help.

"Heck of it is—" He didn't continue until he had dragged himself up the last step and paused as though he needed the time to rally his strength before he took another step or uttered another word. "Every time I look at Eddie and Joanie, I'm back in Marazán."

He sucked in a breath. "My head's like a kaleido-scope. I see flashes of kids like them living in poor lit-tle crowded shacks all over Marazán; the ones who lived in that jungle hut where I dang near died were just about their ages."

His breathing had grown ragged, fast and shallow. Laura could imagine the pain, both physical and emotional, that he must be feeling.

"I—"

Opening the screen door, Laura held it wide as he walked into the store. He seemed to hold on to his words as though taking the few steps that carried him into the cool, dim, old-store-fragrant interior took all his energy. The bell overhead sounded so distant in her ears that it might as well have been on a leather strap around the neck of one of Uncle Zeb's Guernsey cows, in their pasture up the mountain.

Glen must be hurting terribly, and there was noth-ing she could do to help him. She felt awful.

"I keep seeing those hopeless, frightened little faces," he went on, his gaze locking onto hers with an intensity that reached toward her soul. "There's war going on all around them; most of them haven't known anything else in their short lives.

"What the hell's going to happen to them, Laura?" The words seemed wrenched from him. "Marazán's full of kids like them—so damn full it breaks your heart when you know there's nothing you can do. U.S. dollars that should be helping them are lining the pockets of General Mariana or going into Swiss and Bahamian bank accounts. I saw it when I was down there before, three or four years ago, but from what I hear, it's gotten worse, since. So much worse."

When he dragged a breath deep and held it until it seemed his lungs would burst in rebellion, Laura inhaled sharply and promptly thought, Thank God it wasn't audible. Glen wouldn't want her feeling sorry for him. She knew that instinctively.

Shaking his head as though to clear it of a bad memory, Glen muttered, "My head's as messed up as my body," then fell silent.

His face expressed such helplessness that her heart went out to him.

"For a long time," he suddenly continued, "I didn't remember a lot of what happened when the plane crashed, and afterward. Oh, I got nightmares—I still get them—but I didn't remember some of them, only that I'd wake up screaming or wanting to scream but be unable to make a sound. I still don't remember some of them."

Reminding herself of the well-meaning people who had wanted to help her through her grief but hadn't known how, Laura hated herself for just reaching out and touching his arm. She should say something to make the anguish easier for him to bear.

His long fingers combed through his curling black hair, reflecting his frustration. "Hell, Laura," he burst out, "it's been almost eighteen months!"

As if she didn't know.

"I don't know," he muttered, sounding as helpless as she felt. "I remember most of what happened— before the plane crashed, that is. I *think* I remember." Again he shook his head. "I can't even be sure of that. Some of it's fragmented."

"What do the psychologists say?" It was all she could think of.

Except for Frank's message that he had loved her and had wanted to spend his life with her, she didn't want to be reminded of what had happened before the plane went down, or think about what had happened afterward, much less talk about it.

When the plane crashed in Marazán, she had been here on her mountain, waiting for Frank to come for the Christmas holidays, dreaming that *that* would be the time when he would break out of his strong-silent-man mold and tell her how deeply he loved her.

Reminders of the excruciatingly long months since, she didn't need.

"Their stock answer. Same as the others. What else?" Glen's voice brought her out of her unhappy reverie. " 'Give it time.' " A faint grimace—or was it pain? she wondered—flickered over his face when he shrugged. "They're probably right, but I wonder if those kids down in Marazán have time. If time isn't running out for them—"

Abruptly he broke off, then said, "Sorry. I don't mean to keep dredging up memories that hurt you."

Trying to ignore the tremblers the apology sent rolling through her like aftershocks from the emotional quake that had shattered her life, Laura finished the sentence for him "—when Frank's plane was shot down."

The words seemed to come of their own will, in a voice that was so calm it surprised her. How could she sound so normal when she was quivering inside like a leaf in a windstorm?

Also of its own accord, it seemed, her hand closed over his, which grasped the head of his cane, and squeezed it gently. His other hand folded over hers, warm and strong and, she sensed, accepting the compassion she had wordlessly offered.

Sensations she knew she shouldn't permit but was helpless to control coursed up her arm and back again to her palm, leaving her flesh tingling. Was he feeling the same sensations? she wondered. Her heart constricted with the suspicion that he might not be; or if he was, that he interpreted them differently.

"Before that, I suppose."

His voice, although it sounded hoarse and achy, didn't tell her a thing. He was, she thought with a stab of disappointment, too caught up in unpleasant memories of his own to be aware of her, even though his hand still covered hers.

"I was thinking—" he spoke slowly, after a pause "—of the last time I saw those two children in the hut. Or remember seeing them."

Again she remained silent, sure that if she opened her mouth she would spill out the feelings that were in turmoil inside her.

At last he went on. "Eyes as big as saucers in their solemn little faces—standing around staring at me like they thought I was from another planet."

There was a pause. "Every time I drifted awake, later on in the field hospital, if it could be called that, I remembered them, saw their faces swimming in the fog that seemed about to drag me back under, and before long, did."

He paused again. "Although I don't remember being conscious when I was in the hut in the jungle, I guess I must have been, at least some of the time, maybe just drifting in and out again, or I wouldn't have kept seeing their faces."

Listening, with her eyes on his face, Laura sensed a shudder sweeping through him although she saw no outward sign of it.

"Then that day," he continued, "that last day at the hut, one of the guerrillas who carried me out told me later when he came to see me in the hospital that someone came to warn them that the soldiers might be coming. He—the guerrilla—said I told them to leave me. I was dead weight, couldn't lift a finger to help myself and was mumbling half incoherently." The words poured out. "They wouldn't hear of it."

Wincing as though he remembered the pain, he broke off and began to massage his temples with thumb and fingertips, his eyes closed, arousing in her an urge to do it for him.

Shaking himself, he continued. "Funny how clear some things are. Like a jigsaw puzzle. You have some of the pieces, some you don't."

His lean face appeared gaunt in the dim light inside the store where lights hung from the high ceiling. When he didn't go on, Laura spoke softly. "And you can't wait to get back to Marazán and find the rest of the pieces?"

Her heart dove for cover from the hurt she feared his response—and his departure, when the time came—would cause her.

"You got it," Glen replied, although that wasn't quite true. The words—an echo of his terse promise to Carrera in the last moments before the plane crashed—snapped him back through nearly eighteen months' time to the Marazán jungle.

He had been recalling bits and pieces ever since he'd come to in that dinky little hospital in the guerrilla base camp, and now he felt as though a brisk, fresh breeze had blown through his mind—not enough to have totally swept away the cobwebs and the swirling black mists and gray fog that had filled his head ever since he'd lost consciousness facedown in that stinking jungle muck after the plane exploded; but enough to have given him a fair idea of what had happened after Carrera's plane had slammed into the jungle growth at the end of the makeshift airstrip, and enough to show him the wisdom of letting some younger man with the vigor and the drive he'd once had get into the action and finish the story.

Carlos Rodríguez, the Marazán reporter Juan Hernández had sent up to learn the ropes of reporting as it was done in the States and especially in Washington was a sharp kid, besides knowing the ins and outs of Marazán geography and politics. He just might pull it off.

"You're right," he said, daring to let his gaze seek hers again, daring to let himself hope that she would let him into her life in the way he was beginning to feel he wanted to be in it—when this was all over. He couldn't ask her to share what might lie ahead for him, before it was; before he was out of the rat race for good.

But then, he promised himself, *then* . . .

"I have to get that story out," he told her. "Either do it myself, although I don't know if the story can wait for me—the shape I'm in—or let someone else go after it. One way or another, the world has to be told what's happening down there." He finished simply: "I promised Carrera."

She seemed to draw a breath deep into her lungs and hold it for a moment before she exhaled audibly. "If you go, Glen," she managed in a level voice, "it can't be till you're stronger."

She looked infinitely sad, and he knew she was thinking of Carrera. Carrera had been strong, in his prime. But strength—of body, spirit and ideals— hadn't helped him, except, he couldn't help thinking, to die like a man.

But a smile lifted the corners of her mouth, and her eyes seemed to become a deeper blue. Lord, how he wanted to kiss her and hold her, feel her body against his.

The yearning erased the words before they reached his lips.

"Who knows?" she exclaimed, in a low, husky voice, sounding straight off an emotional high. "By then, things may have settled down and no one will have to go."

Thinking that the story would still be there, Glen grinned in spite of the sharp pang of pity that stabbed through him. "Work that miracle and I'll dub you the

Good Witch of the Cumberlands, as well as the bestower of Crane's Cumberland Mountain Magic Therapy.''

"'Bestower'?'' She sounded as though she had it all together now.

"Not that it's apt to happen," he grumbled on. "Politicos in Marazán are an unforgiving bunch when it comes to having their crooked schemes exposed. So are the couple of guerrilla leaders who've been caught with their hands in the same cookie jar. Peace in the country—if by some miracle it were to happen—won't change that."

No, he mused silently, he'd have to figure another way; maybe wangle an assignment for himself to cover U.S. training aid to Honduras, and then arrange for Juan Hernández to meet him—or to meet Carlos, if it turned out Carlos was the one to go—when he sneaked across the border into Marazán.

"Glen—"

Laura's soft voice coaxed him back to reality.

"Sorry," he said apologetically. "I was woolgathering. I came up to make a couple of phone calls. To Sis at Sycamore Point, and John Baz, who's my editor in Washington. They need to know my change in plans."

"Sure," she replied, pointing him toward the phone that sat on a rolltop desk in a rear corner of the store.

Nodding, Glen limped toward the phone, leaning more heavily on his cane than he would have liked. At this rate, he thought, he was a long way from getting to Marazán.

While Glen made his phone calls, Laura puttered around the store, closing up.

Counting the day's receipts and locking the money in the old iron safe beneath the counter didn't take long. Crane's General Mercantile didn't do much business these summer days, outside of the bait and tackle and other supplies stocked mainly for vacationers at the lake. Winters were worse, with more action around the potbellied stove than at the cash register.

Neither did stocking the shelves that had begun to look empty in a few places occupy her for long. Nor did jotting down the few items her grandfather needed to order for delivery by the wholesaler next week when the truck came through from Lexington en route to Lanier, the county seat and nearest town of any size. The supermarket and a new mall in Lanier really cut into the store's business.

Trying not to eavesdrop, however unintentionally, and at the same time keep her mind off her earlier conversation with Glen, Laura retreated to "her" alcove as soon as her chores were done.

Forcing herself to concentrate on deciding which picture to hang in the space left vacant by the painting she had given to Glen wasn't difficult. Sketching and painting were her first loves; losing herself in her work had, she sometimes thought, saved her sanity, these past months.

How long had it been, she wondered, since she had given serious consideration to taking her work off the mountain for shows, except for those that had been scheduled before Frank's accident? She'd forced herself to meet her commitments, but that was all. It hadn't been easy.

"You sure about that, Baz?"

The sound of Glen's voice cracked through the stillness like a bullwhip, bringing Laura around as though she were a top and his taut voice the string that spun her.

He sat at her grandfather's scarred rolltop desk, elbows braced on the worn green blotter amid invoices that her grandfather had left scattered there. Last time she'd looked, he had been rubbing his forehead, his head propped on one hand while the other hand held the phone in what appeared to be a death grip.

Now he sat bolt upright on the edge of the chair, snapped into the position by something he had heard on the phone. Even from across the store she sensed— *saw*—his tension increase further as he listened to what Baz was saying. The editor's booming voice thundered like some distant storm in her ears.

"That can't be." Glen's voice ground out again, like a heel on rough gravel. "Hell, Baz, there's no way anyone could have found out."

He sounded angry, appalled, totally unbelieving of what he'd heard. "Hernández said he was alone in the building when we talked, the other night. *There's no way—*"

Apparently the editor interrupted, although now Laura didn't hear the rumble of his voice, for Glen stopped speaking and appeared to listen intently for a full minute, it seemed.

Finally he muttered something she couldn't hear even though, by then, she was crossing the store toward him.

He hung up and just sat there, his dark head cradled in both hands as though his head suddenly had become detached from his body and he didn't know what to do with it.

Chapter Five

Glen had been conscious of Laura moving around behind him as he'd talked with Baz. Eventually she had gone to the front of the store and let Brewster in.

He'd never been wholly *unaware* of her. But when she asked softly, "What's happened, Glen?" and touched his shoulder lightly, electricity jolted him as though the bullet that had struck down Hernández had ricocheted three thousand miles and zapped him.

He told her, in a hoarse voice that felt as if each word had been torn raw and bleeding from the bottom of his soul, ending up with: "Hernández was the only person besides Frank and me who knew I was on that plane. Baz didn't even know."

She remained silent, her hand still on his shoulder.

"The Hernández family publishes a newspaper in Marazán, the capital city," he went on. "Juan was the editor. You might call him a thorn in the government's side, as his father was, back when Frank's father led an uprising that failed against the military regime that was in power, even then.''

For all that Marazán had been Carrera's native land, Glen didn't know how much she knew of the nation's stormy history. The breath he sucked deep into his lungs reminded him of his recent part in it.

''Two nights ago—'' he exhaled audibly ''—less than an hour after I had talked with him on the phone, Hernández was killed outside the newspaper office. He had called and asked Baz to have me get in touch. Baz called me just before I left Sycamore Point.

''When I got him on the phone—'' the words came slowly ''—he wanted to know when he could expect me back in Marazán.''

''That he'd been killed soon after you'd spoken with him could have been a coincidence.''

She was right. It *could* have been a coincidence. Glen told himself that, tried to convince himself that it was true. The state of affairs in Marazán being what they were, anyone who didn't see eye to eye with the current power structure put his life in jeopardy just by getting out of bed in the morning.

And as editor of the powerful newspaper, Juan Hernández had done a lot more than get out of bed. He had harangued General Mariana, supplied tips to newsmen, been Glen's pipeline right up to the time Glen had been thrown out of the country. On the night of his death Hernández had said there were rumors that Mariana planned to step up the attacks in rural areas.

Coincidence? he asked himself, tasting gall.

No way.

"It wasn't a coincidence," he said quietly, feeling his gut clench.

When would it end?

Laura's arms came around him as he still sat in the ancient swivel chair that, he'd discovered, had a sneaky habit of tilting too far back if he didn't watch it. Her cheek felt soft and warm, pressed against his face.

"You still here, Laura?" Her grandfather's voice boomed from his rooms behind the store.

Glen hadn't heard him come in.

"Yes, Grandpa," Laura called back as they sprang apart, Glen forgetting the treachery of the old chair and very nearly spilling himself backward against her.

"Glen came up to make some phone calls," Laura explained as her grandfather entered the store.

Did she sound flustered? Glen wondered, and felt a surge of disappointment that she hadn't.

"I was just about to suggest getting out the Cherokee and driving him back to the cabin. The way the clouds have rolled in, it's going to be darker than pitch along that trail to the lake—may even rain pretty soon," Laura added.

"It will that," Mason Crane agreed, then inquired, "Sure you won't stay for coffee or a beer, Glen? The rain'll hold off for a while," he predicted, "and even if it doesn't, a little rainstorm never stopped my granddaughter."

Glen shook his head. "Thanks, no."

His gaze locked onto Laura's in spite of his determination that it shouldn't. "And no, thanks, to the offer to drive me down to the cabin, Laura. I need the walk.''

Even if he got caught in the shower that had been threatening when he'd walked up from the lake, he needed the exercise, he thought—for more reasons than one.

How—*now*—could he think of doing anything but going to Marazán himself?

"See you tomorrow," Glen said a little later, as they stood at the store's front door.

Laura nodded.

"About what happened—"

His voice was low. Thank heaven, she thought, although her grandfather had withdrawn discreetly to his rooms.

"It takes two, Glen. Don't apologize."

Where had *that* come from? And with such calm and self-possession, too. She felt warm but not embarrassed. Sliding her arms around Glen and resting her head against his had been too natural—had felt too good—for her to be embarrassed. She only wished Grandpa hadn't chosen that particular moment to come home.

Grinning, Glen said, "I wasn't going to."

Leaning over, he kissed her on the temple. His warm breath fanned tendrils of her hair and spread out to caress her cheek.

She felt kissed all over!

"Night, Laura."

"G'night," Laura whispered back, wondering where her cool presence had gone. Her skin tingled where his lips had brushed. Exciting sensations spun through her, causing her heart to beat faster, her blood to heat up.

She waited until he was safely down the steps and on solid ground before she returned his wave. She watched him limp briskly into the darkness in the direction of the trail that led the short distance down the mountain to the lake before she closed and bolted the door.

When she joined her grandfather in his kitchen—as old-timey as the store—he cocked a grizzled iron-gray brow at her. "Your nose should grow like Pinocchio's, Granddaughter. Getting your four-wheel-drive out to take Glen down to the cabin was the last thing on either of your minds."

His chuckle sounded suspiciously pleased with the scene Laura suspected he had walked in on and then retreated to the kitchen before calling out to her. Grandpa, she thought, would do that, especially if he had instinctively liked Glen. She suspected that he did.

"I been around too long, girl," he continued, his big voice slightly lowered, "not to know a couple of smoochers when I see 'em pretending nothing's going on."

"Now, Grandpa," she protested mildly, feeling her cheeks color. Hoping to change the subject, she asked, "What did Uncle Zeb find out at the clinic, and what have the two of you been doing all this time?"

"You know Zeb and doctors." Which was no answer at all. "Myrtle—" who was Zeb's daughter-in-law "—had supper ready when we got back. I stayed for a bite and a game of checkers."

He answered both questions while peering at her over his glasses. "You like Glen Moran, don't you?"

"Yes."

Walking to the kitchen door, she stood looking at the wooded, rough path that led up the mountain to her little house. If she were there now, she mused, she could watch the storm's approach. Maybe even see Glen's light go on when he reached the cabin on the lakeshore. The thought tickled her senses.

Yes, she liked Glen Moran.

"I like him," she said aloud. "I think I could like him a lot. But—" she paused "—he told me things today, Grandpa, that I'm not sure I can reconcile with."

Breathing in deeply to give herself strength, Laura repeated Glen's words—Frank's request—verbatim. The rest of what Glen had told her she more or less summarized, leaving out his telephone conversation tonight with his editor. Glen could tell Grandpa about his friend Juan Hernández when he wanted to.

"I've got a sick feeling inside," she finished, "that Frank's plane would not have been shot down if Glen hadn't been on board."

Her grandfather took his time pouring himself a glass of milk and returning the jug to the fridge.

"You don't know that, Laura." His lined, weathered face registered concern. "You can't let the past haunt you, the way you've been doing. It'll drive you out of your mind, girl, keep you asking how things happened the way they did, why they happened to someone you loved. You'll only make it worse if you keep thinking the man you may fall in love with might have caused what happened to Frank.''

His gray-haired head wagged reproachfully. ''You can't let your mind dwell on that, honey.''

Laura bit her lip. ''I know that. It's just—''

''Let me finish, Granddaughter. I waited a long time to say this and now that I'm started, I aim to get it said.''

Setting the glass of milk on the table, he pulled out a ladder-backed oak chair almost as old as the store itself, and sat down.

''Frank was a good man, Laura, but he's gone. You can spend the rest of your life grieving and it won't bring him back. It'll only rob you and some other good man—whether it be Glen or another—of a satisfying life together.''

Laura's throat threatened to close up. He was a fine one to talk! Grandma had been gone twenty years and if he had looked at another woman except from across the counter in his general mercantile store, she didn't know about it.

''Goodnight, Grandpa,'' she said, her voice husky with tears that lumped hot and achy and unshed in her throat.

She loved her grandfather dearly—he was the only family she had. It could be that he was all she would ever have, she thought, as loneliness washed over her.

But tonight she didn't want to listen to him being right.

* * *

Rain had fallen during the night, but the sky was clear and mother-of-pearl in the east when Glen woke, famished, at dawn.

After taking a shower as hot as his aching leg and chest and back muscles could stand, he swallowed two aspirin tablets, pulled on jeans and a shirt and went out on the deck. The way his head was pounding, he didn't want to think about the things he knew he must think about.

The lake was a dark blue gem that hadn't yet caught the first light of day. Not a sound that didn't belong to nature broke the stillness. After the hell he had been through, after the thoughts that had tramped heavily through his mind all night, the lake and Crane's Mountain were paradise—almost as serene as Sycamore Point at dawn when a pale mist hung low over the Wabash River.

His stomach growled. Even this early in the morning, the thought of fish rolled in cornmeal before frying teased his senses. But he would have to catch the fish first—and he didn't know, even if he caught them, if there was cornmeal in the kitchen—so he settled for bacon and eggs, English muffins and coffee, which Laura had brought down from the store yesterday.

Laura.

The little sleep he'd gotten last night had been filled with dreams of Laura sandwiched between haunting nightmares about Juan Hernández and Marazán. It had made for a mixed-up night during which he had drifted in and out of sleep, been out of bed almost as much as he'd been in it.

Sighing, he thought that in and out of Laura's arms would have been more like it—and, in and out of the memories of the quasi consciousness he had lain in, more dead than alive, in that piteous little hut in the jungle and later, in one hospital after another until finally, he had wound up in Georgetown University Hospital in Washington, D.C. He'd been there so long that he had started to feel as if the world began in his room and ended in the physical therapy department. Then, the farthest reaches of his universe had been bounded by Washington and the suburbs that huddled around it like baby chicks around a clucking mother hen. Which had been better than what he'd known previously.

Had Hernández been in that little jungle hut? He half remembered—he *thought* he half remembered—having seen the handsome, swarthy face swimming in the dark mist that had seemed to hover over him as he lay semiconscious; half remembered hearing—as though from far away—Hernández's voice, an odd mix of Yale and Spanish accents that had stuck out like a sore thumb in Marazán.

Had he heard Hernández warning the poor *mestizos who lived there to pack up and get out before the soldiers came?*

Had he heard that? Glen wondered, trying to recall the flash of memory, momentarily distinct but then gone again, as he set about clearing away and washing his few breakfast dishes and utensils.

Hernández would have known the soldiers had been on their way. It was the sort of information Hernández conceivably might have come by, given his numerous contacts throughout the country, some even inside the military. Not everyone in Marazán's disproportionately large army was corrupt, but the ones who weren't were in no position to do anything except wait and hope and pray for the coup that might save their country—and pass information to newspapermen like Hernández and Glen Moran at the risk of their own lives, if General Mariana or any of his henchmen should find out.

If so, Glen reflected—if he hadn't imagined Hernández's presence—then Juan Hernández had saved his life, and the lives of the native family that had taken care of him; the lives of the children he couldn't get out of his mind.

What the hell was he going to do now?

Combing his hair, still damp from the shower, with his fingers, Glen pulled on socks and well-worn sneakers he had found in a closet at the house in Sycamore Point during his recuperation there, and returned to the deck.

The small white boat with the triangular yellow sail that he had seen the previous day was out on the lake now, trailing a faint wake that caught the slanting rays of the early-morning sunlight.

Glen smiled to himself when he recognized Laura at the tiller, and Brewster, his broad, shaggy head hanging over the side as though he were fascinated by his own black bearlike image in the water.

The one bright spot in his galaxy, Glen thought.

"Hello-o-o-o!" he yelled.

"Hello, yourself," Laura shouted back, then squealed "Brewster!" when the big dog snapped to attention and plunged into the water, very nearly swamping the little skiff in the process.

Glen laughed and felt a spurt of astonishment that he could chuckle so heartily after yesterday's news. He watched Laura bring the sailboat about and tack toward shore, following more or less in the arrowhead-shaped wake of the paddling dog.

Without going back inside to get his cane, he walked toward the lake, reaching the beach at the same time that Brewster splashed into shallow water.

The dog paused at the water's edge, shook himself vigorously and then rushed toward Glen as though he'd found a long-lost friend, stopping en route to shake himself another time or two.

Laura was grinning broadly when she beached the boat. "You seem to have made a conquest." Amused, Glen suspected, by the sight he presented, she accompanied the words with a shake of her head.

Glen glanced down at himself. Dang dog had done a job on him, all right. He looked, and felt, as though he'd been splashed by an eighteen-wheeler doing eighty down the interstate.

"Not the one I would have preferred making, you can believe me."

Grinning, he felt a surge of pleasure as heightened color washed into her cheeks at his words and the glance that locked onto hers, holding it captive while his senses plundered what he saw there.

"You missed breakfast," he told her when he had gotten his breath back, "but the Good Fairy of the Cumberlands stocked my larder. And I'm pretty good in the kitchen, if I do say so myself. Come on up and I'll fix you up something."

"Will you have a second cup of coffee while I make myself something?"

Her voice, low and husky, a soft Kentucky drawl, wakened a craving inside him. Why did he feel she had trouble breaking eye contact? Was she as attracted to him as he was to her, and last night hadn't been a fluke—two hurt and lonely people reaching out to each other, seeking comfort for their pain, solace for a sorrow they shared?

"Make that a fourth cup—" his raspy voice was a stranger to his own ears "—and you've got a deal."

Furling the small sail with deft movements, Laura said lightly, "You're on."

She leaped out of the skiff with an agility Glen envied and wondered if he would ever possess again.

He looked as though he hadn't slept any better than she had, Laura thought as they walked toward the cabin, she matching her usually brisk, leggy stride to his slower, limping gait. Wondering if the wakefulness had been for the same reason as hers, or was because of his physical pain, she glanced at him, then looked quickly away when she noted the grim set of his jaw. Poor man, did he always hurt?

Instinctively she put out a hand to him, and before she realized what she had done and could take it back, he grasped it, his long fingers curling around hers as though they knew their way intimately.

As though commanded by some force beyond her, her gaze was drawn to his, and she smiled. How warm she felt inside, where she had been cold and empty for so long.

"Do you know how good your hand feels in mine?" His wide mouth, she had told herself as she'd lain awake in the night thinking about him, that would be so generous with a kiss, curved into a broad grin. "How good you felt, last night, in my arms?"

Sensations she had promised herself to control, charged the barricade she had erected around them. She could fall in love with Glen Moran so easily—she *was* falling in love with him, she feared—and she was determined not to.

At least not yet—not until she had things sorted out in her mind.

Last night had been near total disaster in that respect. Usually, after a night spent tossing and turning, she was up at the crack of dawn and off on the mountain, armed with sketch pad and pencils. Early morning was the best time to observe animals and birds. Or she was at her easel. Whichever, she stayed there until some sense of serenity settled into her soul again.

So what was she doing on the lake this morning?

You wanted to see Glen, that's what, her other, sensible self answered. You hoped to find yourself doing exactly what you're doing: touching him, spending time with him.

Conscious of a tremble of desire that she wasn't ready to encourage, she withdrew her hand from his. "Yes."

She hadn't intended for it to come out like that, husky and raspy, making her throat ache. Then why had it? You're twenty-nine years old, Laura Crane. You've been in love. You know how it feels.

But not the way it felt with Glen.

Where had that come from? she asked herself, feeling as though she had stepped into a hole—and, like Alice, had fallen straight down into Wonderland.

Chapter Six

'Help yourself to bacon, eggs, whatever,'' Glen said when they were inside the cabin. Glancing down at his damp shirt and jeans, he added dryly, ''Thanks to your wet dog, I need to wash up and change.''

He disappeared into the bedroom with a grin that left her insides shaking—and her lips curving upward. Brewster had given him a royal welcome, for sure. She liked that, she admitted to herself. Brewster had always been a good judge of character.

In the kitchen alcove she brought bacon, eggs and orange juice from the small fridge, poured herself a glass of the juice and sipped it, then took the skillet down from the rack. Turning on the propane-fueled stove, she placed the skillet on a burner and laid two strips of bacon in it, trying to keep her mind on what she was doing and not on Glen.

It wasn't easy. In fact, it was futile. She had thought about him most of the night. Why stop now?

A few bars of "Listen to the Mockingbird" drifted out of the bedroom, then broke off abruptly as though it had been a while since he had whistled the song—or any other that sounded so spirit lifting.

She knew the feeling, Laura reflected—and promptly chided herself silently that she didn't really know anything about what Glen Moran was experiencing, or about what he had felt during these past few months.

The man had almost died. There'd been two narrow escapes—the second with the fleeing *mestizo* family when they'd abandoned their home barely ahead of Marazán soldiers. He'd had reason to feel low. For that matter, she thought, he still did.

Frowning, she picked up a fork and pushed the sizzling strips of bacon around the skillet. The second narrow escape troubled her: how had the Marazán military known Glen was in that isolated hut?

When she had called the mission after she'd heard the news bulletin that Frank's plane had crashed, no one there had known Glen had been on board. The person she had spoken with had told her, "Surely you are mistaken, Miss Crane. If Mr. Moran had been on the plane, his body would surely have been found. It was not, I can assure you of that. So you must be mistaken."

She frowned at the memory.

Glen was whistling again, in notes as lilting as before, only now and then off-key.

Despite the seriousness of her musing, Laura smiled as she broke two eggs into the skillet and then turned to get out an English muffin from the old-fashioned breadbox that had a little girl picking violets painted on it.

When Glen emerged from the bedroom wearing a dry shirt and jeans and showing no signs of his encounter with a dripping-wet Brewster, she was lifting crisp bacon onto paper towels to drain. The sunny-side-up eggs were already on toasted muffin slices on her plate, which joined her glass of orange juice and cutlery on the small trestle table beside a window.

"If finding you in my kitchen making breakfast is part of Crane's Cumberland Mountain Magic Therapy—" he looked, she noted with a thrill that raced along her nerves, as though he wanted to devour her "—I like the prescription."

Every nerve in her body tingled in response to the trace of hoarseness in his voice. His heated gaze— more a caress than blatant appraisal—roamed over her, leaving a skirl of excitement in its wake.

Forcing a calm she was far from feeling, Laura shook her head smilingly. "The prescription is secret, but I'm not part of it, I assure you."

After pouring two cups of coffee and handing one to him, she carried her own to the table and sat down, marveling that the sensations that rocketed through her didn't cause her to slosh coffee all over her hand. Unfamiliar reactions rolled through her like ocean swells pounding the shore.

How long had it been since she'd felt like this? Not since Frank— No, she confessed to herself, not even then. She had loved Frank, but there hadn't been anything mercurial between them; no surge of emotion such as she felt when she even just thought of Glen.

As Glen seated himself across from her, his knees bumped hers in the space not designed to accommodate two pairs of long legs. Laura felt a spark flare at the brief contact and wondered if he also noticed it. If the shock, like electricity, had exploded through him as it had through her. She didn't dare let her eyes meet his, no matter how much trouble she had keeping her eyes on her plate.

Trying not to appear flustered, she sliced the side of her fork into an egg on a muffin and managed to get the bite to her mouth without dropping it.

"Bet you," Glen remarked, "the guy who built this table was five-six, tops."

Something in his voice impelled her gaze to leap to his face. He wasn't laughing at her, he wasn't even smiling, but an intensity in his dark brown eyes fanned the flame that had been smoldering deep inside her almost from the moment they'd met.

"Mr. Sears or Mr. Roebuck?" she suggested.

Lord love her, how could she be so discombobulated by a man she'd known less than twenty-four hours? *She*, who had always been so in control of her life where men were concerned.

Grinning, Glen lifted his coffee mug and took a swallow. His eyes never left her face. A pleasing warmth trailed in the wake of his glance, electrifying her senses.

Both of Glen's hands unfolded from around the mug of steaming coffee and reached for her. Framing her face with his hands, he drew her gently toward him as he leaned across the narrow table.

Unable to resist, she met him halfway, her heart racing. Blood pounded in her ears like distant, low-rumbling thunder far away in the mountains. She'd never felt like *this*.

Gently his mouth covered hers, his tongue moving slowly, sensually, over her lips. Hers ventured to meet his.

How good he tasted, of mint and coffee and something more—a musky flavor she couldn't define but which made her want more.

After the tender, hungry caress, he lifted his mouth from hers but still held her face in the embrace of his faintly abrasive palms. They weren't at all the hands of a man who'd spent months in hospitals. He must have worked with his hands during his recuperation at Sycamore Point, she thought involuntarily as his long fingers thrust into her hair and moved against her scalp as though he were inscribing his passion onto her brain.

"Now I know what Crane's Cumberland Mountain Magic Therapy means," he whispered hoarsely. Cradling her face between his hands, he explored her mouth again with his questing, savoring tongue.

"I told you," Laura murmured when she could. "I'm not part of the magic."

"For me, you are."

Rattled, she stabbed a piece of bacon with her fork and then, when it flew apart beneath the nervous assault, picked up a piece and nibbled at it. Without looking at him.

She wasn't, she told herself sternly, about to be Crane's Cumberland Mountain Magic for Glen. She couldn't afford to let herself become important to him, or let him become too important to her. Only heartbreak lay that way, and she couldn't handle it again.

"Glad you're big on breakfast," he said after a long moment's silence. "Breakfast's always been my main meal."

How he wanted to trace the line of her jaw with his fingertips, let the glow that seemed to surround her like some psychic aura warm him, erase the specters of Marazán and Juan Hernández that haunted him.

"Lets me skip lunch—" the sound of his own voice startled him, it was so strained "—without starving half to death if I get tied up on a story."

"Does that happen often?" She dabbed at her lips with a napkin.

Obviously, he decided, she was trying as hard as he to get the focus back to casual. With an effort he got a handle on his emotions. Concentrating on filling coffee cups was a poor substitute for looking at her!

"Often enough. Usually I ended up so danged ashamed of eating well when everywhere I looked I saw half-naked kids watching every bite that I couldn't swallow."

As though suddenly unable to swallow herself, Laura pushed her plate away. "Was it that way in Marazán?"

Setting the percolator down on the end of the table, he resumed his seat, folding his long legs under the table, this time taking care not to bang his kneecaps against hers—and missed the thrill that had leaped through him at the earlier contact.

"Sure you want to hear about Marazán?" He didn't want to tell her—she had been hurt enough by what had happened to Carrera without being reminded of it. *He* had been hurt enough by that stinking little banana republic; given enough of himself to it to write off any bad Karma he might be carrying around.

"You're going back." The glance she gave him was level, unsmiling, but soft as melted butter. So was her voice when she continued. "Yes. Yes, I'm sure. I . . . Glen, I need to know."

Lifting his cup, Glen gulped coffee while he regained control. "It's going to be a long summer if you keep looking at me like that." Marazán, he decided, might be a safer subject.

"Looking at you how?"

She sounded cucumber cool, but a telltale pink that flared momentarily across her cheeks hinted that she wasn't; that she was as shaken by what had happened between them—was still happening between them—as he.

"The way you looked at me just now. Like you'd lost something in my soul and were searching for it."

The way, he thought without meaning to, he had been searching—perhaps all his adult life, without realizing it—for a woman to love, a woman who would love him, give him the kind of peace within himself that he'd always sensed his father had known with his mother; a woman to grow old along with him . . . and to share the good and the bad along the way.

In some place like Sycamore Point—or Crane's Mountain, Kentucky.

Laura.

Surprise, and amusement, and then something she couldn't quite define, flickered across his face. "Why, Glen Moran!" she exclaimed softly. "I do believe you're a romantic!"

Grinning, Glen confessed, "Never said I wasn't." The grin broadening, he added, "I also bring home lost dogs and birds with broken wings."

The expression he hadn't been able to decipher before was back on her face, turning her eyes a deeper blue, giving her that glow that lit the cabin like the morning sun; a glow so real that he felt its heat.

"What," she began, her voice as soft as before, "were you thinking about just now?"

The question—the way she asked it, with her gaze locked onto his—jolted him. What would she say if he told her he was thinking of letting young Rodríguez do the Marazán story while he settled down on Crane's Mountain with her? To finish his book, to fall deeper into love with her? To nurture the kind of relationship he'd always felt his parents had enjoyed with each other?

And also, why he couldn't do any of that until he had this last story from Marazán wrapped up, no matter how close to heaven a life with Laura could be.

Why the hell couldn't his life finally come together?

"Hey," called a soft voice from the deck at the front of the cabin, "y'all ready for company in there?"

"Jo," Laura murmured before Glen recognized Jo Lewellyn's Georgia drawl.

Thinking it sure was easy to see where Joanie and Eddie got their knack for bad timing, Glen called back, "Sure. Come on in. You're in time for breakfast if you don't mind eating the third shift."

Watching Jo pull the screen door open and stand back for Brewster to enter first, he decided that "Brewster first" was protocol around here. Reminded of Fruitful and her pups at Sycamore Point, he thought that Brewster sure accepted the courtesy as his due. Plume waving, the dog beelined for Laura, who slipped him a piece of muffin sopped in egg yolk.

"Would you believe I had breakfast an hour ago?" Jo laughed. "Those kids of mine—"

Sobering, she broke off abruptly, then continued in a more serious tone. "Glen, there was a call for you up at the store. From a Mr. Baz in Washington, D.C. He wants you to call him back as soon as you can. Uncle Mason sent me to fetch you."

The fist that hadn't quite left Glen's gut since he had talked to the editor last night clenched tighter.

"Don't say it," Laura warned her friend when Glen, whom they had accompanied to the store, had disappeared inside.

"Who says I was about to say anything?"

Jo wore the characteristic cocked-eyebrow expression that Laura knew so well—a clear indication that Jo wouldn't believe anything Laura could tell her to explain the innocence of her being in Glen's cabin at this hour of the morning, even if it were sworn to on a stack of Bibles. So why should she bother with any sort of denial?

"Nobody has to," Laura answered, feeling a smile creep up on her. *Totally* innocent?

She and Jo Lewellyn had been friends ever since Eddie had brought Jo home to Crane's Mountain as his bride after their Atlanta wedding. And, Laura realized, Jo could read her like a book.

"It's written all over you," Laura told her friend.

Jo gave her an impish grin. "You almost never take the skiff out anymo— Sorry, Laura. Guess I'm not thinking this morning. I didn't mean to remind you."

"Forget it." Laura heaved a sigh. "I've thought so much about Frank since Glen came yesterday that one more reminder won't make me hurt any worse."

The few times he had visited Crane's Mountain, Frank had loved taking the little skiff out, saying he couldn't believe how free he felt when he was out on the lake—almost as free as when he was flying, he'd said. It was only natural that Jo would remember.

"Hey, I know." Jo's emerald eyes sharpened. "What did Glen come for, anyhow? I didn't know you two even knew each other."

"We don't—we didn't. But he's still in therapy, sort of. He's been recuperating at his home in Sycamore Point, up in Indiana, and going back to the hospital in D.C. every few weeks."

Getting a grip on her emotions, Laura explained the reason for Glen's visit, ending with "And then, last night, he learned that his contact in Marazán had been murdered." She inhaled deeply. "Did you see his face when you told him John Baz had called again? I wonder what terrible thing has happened now."

Surprising Laura, Jo remained silent as they climbed the worn wooden steps to the porch and entered the store. Jo wasn't given to keeping her thoughts to herself, especially when a friend was hurting.

Glen was seated again at the old rolltop desk at the back of the store, leaning on his elbows among invoices, as he'd done last night. Only now, he was drumming the desktop with the fingers of his free hand, not clutching the phone as though he feared his very life depended on it.

He looked so grim—and so angry. The scar across his temple stood out even more lividly than usual against his tan.

"Get me back down there!" The words ground out, coarse grist from the mill of his fury. "No, I don't want you to send Rodríguez.... I know I did, but not now!" Glen snapped after a pause. "Hernández was my friend—yes, I know Carlos is a good reporter.... I know that, too!"

There was another silence, but brief—and charged. Then Glen burst out, "Well, see what you can do!"

"No," Laura whispered, more to herself than to Jo, who stood beside her at the entrance to the alcove filled with her paintings and sketches. Glen wasn't physically ready. He wouldn't be—not for weeks, maybe months; not even with Crane's Cumberland Mountain Magic Therapy to help him.

Where had that come from? Crane's Cumberland Mountain Magic Therapy was a mythical nostrum that

Glen had concocted to tease her because she'd told him she believed the serene beauty of the mountains ha helped her through her own sorrow....

"Just *do* it!" Glen rasped out the words in r sponse to something Baz had said. "I'll be ready. I' get ready, damn it! Just get back to me!"

Although she hadn't been conscious of havin moved, Laura was beside him when he slammed dow the phone and just sat there, as though he were to stunned by what he had heard to move.

Her heart going out to him, she asked quietl' "What is it, Glen?"

As if it were the most natural thing in the world f him to do, he reached for her hand and folded both o his around it. Her heart constricted.

"Hernández's newspaper, his home, and the U.S aid mission were bombed during the night." His voi was hoarse, strained.

"Oh, Glen," she whispered. Inhaling deeply, sh asked, "Was...anyone killed or injured?" He had tol her last night that Hernández had left a family.

Shaking his head, he said, "Fortunately, no. H wife, Isabelle, received a telephoned warning, and sh and the children and the housekeeper got out in tim At that hour of the night both the newspaper buil ing and the relief agency were empty, thank God."

Releasing her hand, he used both of his to lev himself out of the ancient swivel chair and looke around for his cane. Laura retrieved it from the floc and silently handed it to him.

He's going back, she thought, and I can't stop hir She wasn't sure she wanted to. Glen was Glen, an that was why she loved him—for being the caring and sensitive and courageous man that he was.

But she'd be damned, she told herself, if she would help him get ready to fly off to meet his destiny. She would, she supposed, do as she'd done before with Frank: see him off with a kiss and a smile, and then wait and hope and pray and die a little bit each day until he was safely home.

Chapter Seven

Spindrift off white water that churned over and around rocks in the bed of the small stream glinted in brilliant sunlight, creating an illusion of jewels being tossed by playful, unseen hands into the sweet, clear air.

As always happened when she saw such beauty Laura's imagination caught fire. Her fingers itched for pencil or brush, her hands for sketch pad or palette.

"This is where you painted the picture you gave me, isn't it?" Glen asked.

"Yes." Laura nodded. "Johnny Lewellyn, Eddie Senior's youngest brother, posed for me. On that big rock," she added, pointing toward a boulder on the far side of the narrow, shallow stream.

"Rough water like that doesn't look like much of a fishing spot."

Smiling, Laura said lightly, "But a great setting for a painting, don't you think?"

"I was about to say that." Glen grinned back.

Wiping a thin sheen of sweat from his forehead and then drying his palm on the seat of his cutoff jeans, he asked, "How about a breather?"

"Thought you'd never ask."

Exaggerating a sigh, she plopped down on the lush grass and stretched her long, slender legs as far as they would go. Nudging her moccasins off, she wiggled her bare toes.

The sun felt delicious, the light breeze delectable. The day was so beautiful she could taste it. If she could choose her final day on earth, it would be a day like this one, she told herself, so she could carry the memory with her into eternity.

"You set a wicked pace today," she accused lightly, to get her mind off the exciting sensations created by being so near to Glen.

It didn't work. Glen beside her led her thoughts on to all sorts of tangents, but the reason behind all his excursions along mountain trails still lurked behind every rock and tree and turn in their path: *Marazán.*

He'd been hard at it for three weeks, since he had learned of Juan Hernández's death and the bombings of the man's newspaper and home and the United States relief agency in Marazán. Walking, swimming, calisthenics—sometimes with her, but more often alone or accompanied by Brewster.

The result was evident. He walked with less of a limp, laying his cane aside more and more often and for longer periods of time. Steep trails now left him less winded than the walk up from the lake had at first. His tan had deepened from being out in the sun so much.

Even the livid scar that slashed across his temple and disappeared into his unruly black hair, and the jagged reminders of thigh and chest and back wounds, appeared less angry than before.

Completing her visual examination as thoroughly as possible without giving in to the tingling excitement in her fingertips and exploring the zigzag scar that plunged from under his denim cutoffs down the inside of his left thigh, Laura forced her thoughts elsewhere.

It wasn't easy. Blood pounded louder in her ears than the rush of white water. She felt uncomfortably warm, and she knew that the temperature of the July day had nothing to do with it. Summer in the high Cumberlands, though sometimes hot, so far had been unusually pleasant.

No—the thought began in spite of her determination not to think about Glen—the undue warmth that assailed her came from Glen, who had seated himself beside her. Lying back, he folded his arms under his head. As though from a tropical storm brewing inside her, heat seemed to envelop her.

All six-feet-two of Glen's lean frame tantalized her senses, shattered her control. She wanted nothing more than to lean over him, fuse her mouth to his, feel his hands in her hair holding her while their tongues wooed each other's mounting passion.

Who wooed *whose* mounting passion? she asked herself derisively.

Glen hadn't made a romantic move toward her since that first morning at the cabin, and the way he was— so wrapped up in getting himself into physical shape to go back to Marazán—he wasn't apt to.

And, with him so determined to get back into the rebellion-torn little country, she wasn't going to let herself fall into love with him.

So what was she thinking?

Drawing her knees up, she folded her arms around them and buried her face there, letting her hair tumble down to hide the warmth she felt rushing over her. Surely she was blushing from the top of her head to the tips of her toes.

"Laura—" Glen's voice was a hoarse whisper, sensual in her ears.

She had to tell him how she felt....

Unaware of his having moved, she suddenly realized his hands were on her shoulders, and his lips were on her nape, where her hair had parted when she had leaned forward to hide her face.

"Hey! It's Glen and Aunt Laura!"

This was followed by the inevitable gleeful echo, "Hey!"

At the sound of the Lewellyn children's voices, Laura and Glen sprang apart.

"Somebody ought to put a bell around those kids' necks." Glen's growl, half under his breath, sounded so good-natured that Laura had to smile.

"Hi," she greeted the children. "I thought you'd gone back to Atlanta."

Jo had said goodbye yesterday, saying she had to get back to work. "Gotta keep the wolf from the door, you know."

Which was a laugh, Laura knew for a fact. Eddie Lewellyn may have taken one risk too many on a fast track and gotten himself killed, but he had been a loving and thoughtful man who had left his family well-off financially. Jo, she was sure, wouldn't have to work if she didn't want to.

"We're gonna stay with Gramma and Grampa till school starts." Joanie's glance, first at Glen and then back to Laura, was openly speculative, Laura noted.

How much had they seen? she wondered, feeling the rush of returning warmth on her face. She still felt Glen's brand, the shape of his mouth, on her nape. It should have been singeing her hair.

"I'm gonna be in kindergarten."

"Kindergarten's fun," Glen said, and Laura saw him wink at Eddie as though they shared a secret. "Remind me sometime and I'll give you some pointers."

"Kindergarten's boring," Joanie scoffed.

"What's a pointer?" Eddie wanted to know, his wide eyes on Glen.

Grabbing her brother's hand, Joanie whispered, "C'mon. Can't you see they want to be alone, dummy? Let's go play in our cave!"

"All right!"

Like agile young woods creatures, they scaled the rock seemingly as easily as they had descended it.

Shaking his head, Glen asked, "What cave are they talking about? Is it safe?"

Laura smiled. "As a church. It's on the Lewellyn farm, a shallow hole in rock, really. Their father and his brothers and I played in it when we were kids, pretending we were Daniel Boone and the settlers hiding from wild Indians. Sometimes—" she grinned "—I got to be an Indian."

Smiling, Glen got to his feet with more agility than he could have a week ago, Laura noted, and gave her a hand up.

When he kept her hand in his, a thrill leaped through her in spite of all the admonishments against such sensations that she had imposed.

Meshing his fingers with hers, he suggested, "Tell me about your childhood." His grin broadened. "Daniel Boone and the Indians. Everything."

"If you'll tell me about yours."

"Deal. But you go first."

Laura smiled and began, the rushing white water murmuring accompaniment.

She'd never, she realized, felt so close to him.

Was it possible that the sense of caring, the loving, the consuming need she felt to share wasn't something only *she* felt?

"Had a call for you a while ago, Glen," was Mason Crane's booming greeting when Laura and Glen arrived at the store after leisurely following the whitewater stream all the way to its confluence with the placid lake, not far from Glen's cabin.

The day's pleasantness suddenly seemed threatened—even more threatened than when they had talked of her feelings about his return to Marazán. He had spoken earlier of letting the young Marazánian, Carlos Rodríguez, who was on the Washington newspaper's Central American desk, go instead of him. But Juan Hernández's death and the subsequent fire-bombings seemed to have hardened Glen's resolve to go himself.

A chill skirled through Laura as her grandfather continued speaking to Glen. "Mr. Baz called to say your doctor at Georgetown University Hospital wanted to be sure you don't forget your checkup."

"Yeah, I know. I hadn't forgotten. Thanks."

He hadn't forgotten, but he hadn't mentioned it, either. And he'd had ample opportunity today; they had talked about so much in their lives. Laura felt vaguely disappointed.

But, she realized, she should have anticipated a follow-up examination to assess his progress. Anyone who had been through such an ordeal—who'd had orthopedic surgeons and physical therapists all over him for so long—would face checkups till the cows came home.

"When?" she asked, feeling as though she might choke on the word before she heard his answer. It was the beginning of the end of Glen's stay at Crane's Mountain—perhaps the end of his stay in her life. She could feel it.

If reports were good, he might not come back at all—he might not *want* to come back.

A relationship needed more than a kiss on the neck, more than a kiss shared across a breakfast table, more than companionship; more than reminiscing about their childhoods; more even than the friendship she sensed was deepening and strengthening between them; more than the wild rush of warmth and compassion she had felt for him when he'd come home carrying the baby raccoons he had found trying to nurse from their dead mother in the middle of the highway.

Certainly it needed more than memories of Marazán and the man whose death had brought them together, she thought—and wished she hadn't. That part of her life was behind her. It was the first time, she realized, that she had admitted that, even to herself.

"Next week," Glen answered, finally.

Hooking his cane on the edge of the counter beside the cash register, he fished coins from a pocket and limped over to feed them into the soft-drink machine.

"The usual?" he asked as the quarters rattled down the change tube.

When she nodded, he pressed a bar and caught the can as it came out of the machine. Pulling the tab, he handed the drink to her, almost in one deft motion.

Taking it, Laura felt a smile tug at the corners of her mouth as she murmured "Thanks." There was no reason she should enjoy watching every ordinary move he made, but she did.

Trying not to think how much she was going to miss him, she waited until he had leaned forward to catch his own can of cola as it popped from the machine before she spoke. "Why don't I come to D.C. with you? I could visit the gallery and talk about the arrange—"

"No!" The word exploded from his lips.

"—ments for my show," she finished valiantly.

What was wrong with him? They'd talked a lot about the one-woman show she had begun to plan at the prestigious gallery in Washington that had shown her work before. He'd thought it a great idea, he had said; time she was getting on with her life and her career. He had even offered to loan her his *Boy Fishing*. "If you promise not to sell it out from under me," he had added.

And now "No!" as though she had suggested he pose for her nude on the Capitol steps?

"I don't understand," she said quietly, placing her cola on the counter without tasting it. "I thought you could show me your Washington."

"You wouldn't like the Washington that's going to be mine this time around."

Grimly he gulped his drink, clutching the aluminum can so hard that Laura expected it to crumple in his fist, spewing cola all over.

"Can't you let me be the judge of that?"

Vaguely Laura heard her grandfather say something about "goin' out to set a spell with Zeb," who as usual was taking the sun on the store's front porch, and then the sound of the old cowbell over the door, confirming his departure.

"Not this time, love."

Laura's heart skipped a beat. He had called her "love." But so casually, naturally; as if the thought of her being his love had become a given with him and he hadn't realized what he was saying. She was afraid to let herself think so.

Needing desperately to do *something*, she reached for her can of cola. His hands stopped her.

"I shouldn't have said that," he muttered apologetically, his voice faintly rough. His fingers closed over hers, curled against her palm.

"'Love'?" The word was a soft, husky syllable, sensuous in her own ears, tasting incredibly sweet on her tongue. She couldn't believe the sensations that charged through her.

Nodding, he placed his cola can down beside hers. For a moment he appeared to study the trickles of condensed moisture that slid down the shiny aluminum onto the smooth wood of the counter. Then, as though returning from another world, he heaved a sigh.

"Coming here was a mistake."

A mistake? How could he say that? *Mean that?* Her heart plummeted. In a near whisper she repeated, "Can't you let me be the judge of that?"

Glen released her hand as though the touch of her flesh against his had burned him. "'Fraid not."

He suddenly sounded so pragmatic that she wanted to shake him—if that was the only way she could touch him.

He thrust his long-fingered hands into his back pockets. A safe place for them? Laura wondered, daring to dream that his feelings matched her own— that he was as hungry to touch her as she was to feel his hands on her body, loving her.

"When I finally found you—" his gaze roamed her face "—the smart thing would have been to have gone back to Brownsville and asked Carmelita to come see you.

"You two are all Carrera had—you need to get to know each other," he interjected, although, Laura mused, she didn't know why he should say that, or feel that way.

Frank hadn't talked to her about his family, or about much else in his life. She had known he was from Marazán, that when he had been ten years old his family had fled to the United States. And she knew a little—a very little—about his time in Vietnam. The rest he had kept locked inside himself.

Sometimes she had wondered—and had asked herself each time where the doubt had come from—how she could have been so attracted to a man who had shut her out of so much in his life.

"Carmelita," Glen continued when she didn't speak, "could have given you Carrera's message." Hoarseness tinged his voice.

Laura's throat threatened to close up. "I'm glad I heard it from you."

"So am I."

With a near silence between them, they packed a picnic of cheese and crackers and fruit and cola and carried the basket up the trail that led to Laura's house on the ridge that rose above the store.

It was a hard climb for Glen, Laura suspected, even though he had made good progress since his arrival on Crane's Mountain. The magic of the mountain seemed to be working for him, as it had worked for her, she reflected as she led the way.

When they reached the small plateau on which her little aerie was perched, overlooking the mountains and the valleys she loved, he gazed around them. He was breathing deep and, she noted with a dash of sympathy, hard.

"I'm bushed," he admitted, "but the view's worth it." Gulping air, he gripped the head of his cane as though it had suddenly become important to him.

Pretending not to notice, she said, "You should see it in winter, when there's snow."

"Bet it's beautiful." He let his eyes roam. "I'd like to show you Sycamore Point in all the different seasons. Winter's special there, too. Maybe, when I'm back, we can go."

"Maybe we can," she whispered. Her grip on the handles of the picnic basket tightened. "Do you have to go, Glen? You said yourself that Carlos Rodríguez is a good reporter and that he has worked in Marazán City. Surely—" Her heart, pleading with him, was in her voice.

"I owe those people!" His tone was harsh. "Juan Hernández. Carrera. The people who saved my life."

"You owe yourself, too," she broke in softly, fighting rising emotion. "Look at you, you nearly died!" The words rushed out although she struggled to slow them, to control the surging emotion that roiled inside her. How could he be so blind?

She loved him. She didn't want to lose him.

Before those words formed on her lips and rushed out, too, Glen took the basket from her and placed it on the broad railing that bordered the deck at the front of her house.

"Come here, love...."

Chapter Eight

Glen had suspected before he saw the grim set of Baz's jutting chin that the sense of euphoria that had been with him since he'd called Laura after leaving Georgetown University Hospital a couple of hours earlier was too good to last.

When Baz growled "Close the door, Glen, and sit down," he was sure of it.

Wondering what was about to hit the fan, Glen winked at the editor's grandmotherly secretary who had lifted a brow when she'd heard their boss's rumbled order, and shut the door.

He hadn't checked in with Baz since he'd gotten into town five days ago.

Between the time of that conversation and his admission to the hospital, he had spent three days rattling cages and looking under rocks. The day and a half he'd spent in the hospital had given the State Department and the Marazán Embassy plenty of time to come down on Baz; and judging from the look on the editor's chiseled-in-stone face, somebody had come down—hard.

Bracing himself, Glen crossed the room in three limping strides and sat down. The limp, the orthopedist had told him, would be with him "awhile," which wasn't the greatest news he could have heard.

"What's the verdict?" Baz asked, his deep voice gruff with what Glen knew was genuine concern; the newspaper's editorial staff was Baz's family.

"Good as new."

Glancing away, Baz punched a key that cleared the VDT screen at his elbow of what Glen had recognized as the opening of an editorial boldly headlined "Marazán."

Before Glen could ask what currently was going on that had inspired the editorial, Baz said, "Don't get antsy and mess things up."

"Okay."

Shrugging, Glen realized with a start of surprise that the shifting of muscles in his shoulders and back no longer had him feeling as though he were on the rack with a medieval executioner tightening the screws.

"Make it 'next to good as new,'" he confessed. "That's what a couple of the doctors said."

"So Ross—" who was one of the orthopedists "—told me at dinner last night," Baz put in. "As I recall, 'six to eight weeks of Crane's Cumberland Mountain Magic Therapy' was what he said." A smile twisted Baz's bulldog face. "I don't suppose you'd like to explain that?"

"You suppose right," Glen answered, feeling goo
all over again.

For the nth time since he'd left her, he wished h
had brought Laura to D.C. with him. They could hav
had a great time—even though Laura's presence woul
have been a constant reminder that she thought he wa
playing Russian roulette with his life by going back t
Marazán. As his jaw tightened, he admitted to him
self that she was right.

But he still had to go.

"Ross," the editor began again, "also said he wan
to see you again in September." He fixed a steady loo
on Glen. "We'll talk reassignment after that."

Glen had known that was coming, and started t
launch his campaign: "The story can't wait anoth
two months. Let's talk assignment now. There's a gu
over at State who thinks he can get me cleared to go i
undercover as a third assistant to the ambassador
aide, or something. I can be on my way in—"

"I know all about your man at State." Baz sounde
at once stern and understanding. "His game pla
wouldn't fool an old hand at the game like Marian
and both you and he know it. But let that go for th
moment." A sigh whistled out from deep in the ed
tor's lungs. "There's a lot going on that you don
know about."

The breath whistled back in. "Much as I'd like
blow the general out of the water with your story o
the front pages for a week, we can't risk letting you g
back to Marazán now. We couldn't—even if Ross ha
discharged you today as fit."

Scowling, Glen said, "You lost me."

He knew his editor well. Baz didn't usually balk at risks. The top-notch editor had once been a sharp reporter who'd taken plenty of risks himself.

No, Glen decided, something was very definitely up—something besides the wild hare's dream he'd tossed at the State Department man the last time they'd talked; also something besides the possibility he and Baz already had discussed: sending Rodríguez instead of him.

He waited, glad he hadn't told Baz the idea for getting back into Marazán as a member of the diplomatic staff had been his own and hadn't originated with his "man at State." Baz took a dim view of his reporters doing anything that conceivably might get them labeled "spies."

"How long has it been since you talked with Isabelle Hernández?" the editor demanded, when the silence between them had grown long.

The question startled Glen. "Two or three days after Juan's funeral. She and the kids were with Juan's mother at the house in the suburbs." Alarm percolated through him. "Why?"

Before he spoke again, Baz spent several seconds studying the steeple he had made by placing his blunt fingertips together. It was a signal, Glen knew from long association with the veteran editor, that Baz was deeply troubled.

"Some newspaper friends are trying, with the State Department's help, to get Isabelle and the children out of Marazán."

Glen frowned to himself. He had met Isabelle Hernández. He liked her. He didn't want anything happening to her.

"As Juan's widow," Baz continued, speaking although each word were heavier than the one that had preceded it, "Isabelle is considered by some to have become Marazán's conscience."

"Marazán doesn't have a conscience," Glen muttered, his tone hard.

The mailed fist that, these past few weeks, had all but vanished along with the worst of the nightmares, slammed into his gut. Suddenly he felt raw and bleeding and aching inside, as emotionally shredded as he had been when he'd arrived in the Cumberlands and given himself over to Laura's mountain magic.

Juan Hernández might well have been murdered because of him—certainly, Juan had died within hours of their conversation that night three weeks ago. *He owed Isabelle Hernández and her children.*

"Whoa. Wait a minute." With an effort Glen got his mind back on track. "You said you're *trying* to get them out. What does that mean?"

The editor dragged in a breath. "Isabelle has been refused a visa to travel outside the country. Three days ago, Señora Marguerita Hernández, Juan's mother, went to the United States Consulate in Marazán city and reported her daughter-in-law and the children missing."

Ignoring Glen's muttered expletive, the editor continued. "They had gone for a drive in the country. They didn't come back, Señora Hernández reported. The car was found the next day near a crossing of the

Misión River, perhaps fifteen miles from the medical mission you and Carrera were headed for when Carrera landed the plane in the arms of one of Mariana's roving patrols."

"That," Glen grumbled protestingly, "wasn't exactly by choice."

Baz grunted. "Government patrols have been reported to be stepping up action in the area lately."

Glen considered that, frowning. It wasn't a good sign. From the sketchy news he'd heard from Marazán over the past year and a half, the rural areas had become the guerrillas' last hope.

Isabelle, he thought, was going to have to be more than her country's "conscience" if Marazán was to survive and again become the democracy it had once been. But first, she needed to get out of the country; needed a power base in a friendly country from which to rally support—

Good God, what was he thinking?

"If they managed to reach the mission," he began, and then realized he was grasping at straws—and stopped.

What lone woman in her right mind would take on Mariana and his army—would try to escape a military dictatorship—with three small children under five in tow? For all that she had stood strong beside Juan Hernández, Glen had trouble conjuring a picture of her in the jungle and higher mountain country on a dangerous run for the border.

No. She had to have been kidnapped.

"So what—" he forced himself to go on "—do we do now?"

"We wait. And we pray." Baz heaved a ragged sigh. "A little Moran's luck wouldn't hurt."

Shoving himself to his feet, the editor came around the desk, hand outstretched to grasp Glen's as he, too, stood up.

"Go back to your dispenser of magic, Glen. Give her my best, and tell her I expect to be invited to the wedding." The handclasp tightened. "Don't let yourself think of anything else."

If only he could manage that, Glen thought.

If only the specter of Mariana's soldiers in camou garb alongside the makeshift runway hacked out of the jungle by friendly *mestizos* from the mission to receive Carrera's plane hadn't risen to haunt him; and all but push his vision of Laura—the feel of her in his arms—out of his mind.

God in heaven, he thought as he made his way out of the newspaper building by the quickest possible route, what would happen to Isabelle if Mariana's soldiers had waylaid her at the isolated river crossing?

He didn't want to think about it.

General Mariana wasn't known for his compassion toward enemies of his regime—even when the enemy was a beautiful woman.

Nor was he known for encouraging it in his troops.

While his car was being serviced for the trip home— strange, he mused, how quickly he had come to think of the tiny cabin on Crane's Mountain as "home"— Glen called his contact at the State Department from a pay phone.

Using pay phones was a habit he'd slipped into long ago when he'd found his apartment phone bugged one time too many. Although he had managed to salvage the story he'd been working on at the time, it had been too close for comfort. Since then, he'd used his apartment phone mostly to order pizza, even though he had it checked regularly for listening devices.

"Where are you?" was his contact's first question when Glen identified himself.

"My version of a safe phone. In a booth on a street corner. I just left Baz. Would you care to give me the inside scoop on what's going on?"

"You know I can't do that without jeopardizing the subjects."

"Stop talking about them as though they're rutabagas, damn it! I owe those people, and I intend—"

"Don't even *think* it. That harebrained scheme of yours set the secretary on his ear. He's not ready for anything else—uh—creative from you."

The quiet, smooth manner came across the wire unruffled, as placid as the lake in front of the cabin on a windless day. Why, Glen wondered, wasn't he reassured?

"Let us do our job. For once—" the oddly unreassuring voice that Glen wanted to believe dropped to a confidential near whisper "—we seem to be doing something right down there."

"Sure as hell," Glen muttered, "you'd better be."

"You'll be the first to know."

Oh, yeah. Sure, Glen thought. He'd heard that before—and then had gotten the story along with a roomful of other reporters hastily summoned to a news conference. Which probably had been broadcast live on national TV, leaving him and the rest of the print media holding the bag.

"By the way—" the unctuous State Department voice seemed to have hardened a tad "—General Mariana knew you were aboard Carrera's plane last December before you cleared the runway at Miami International. What makes you think you stand a chance of getting inside Marazán now and pulling off what you're considering?"

Trying to ignore the old familiar clenching in his gut, Glen snapped, "As of now I'm not considering anything." How could he, when he might jeopardize the lives of Isabelle Hernández and her children? "I'm heading back to God's country, otherwise known as Crane's Mountain, Kentucky, and praying my damn head off that you know what you're doing."

And, he could have added, letting Crane's Cumberland Mountain Magic repair the damage that less than five days in Washington had done to his psyche.

"When I was a young'un—"

Hearing Uncle Zeb's equivalent of "Once upon a time," Laura leaned back against one of the rough-hewn posts on the store's front porch and smiled to herself. Perfect. Joanie and Eddie Lewellyn would be captivated for the next hour, at least, by another of Uncle Zeb's stories.

She'd heard them all before, in her own childhood; but in a way she envied the children who were hearing the stories for the first time. Uncle Zeb was a born storyteller who often got as carried away by the tales he spun as did his young listeners.

Not bothering to be secretive—they wouldn't pay any attention to her, anyway—she opened her drawing pad to the sketch she'd already roughed out: the old man in his rocking chair, the children seated cross-legged in front of him, the big black dog.

Now, if she could capture the rapt expressions on the kids' faces, the look of nostalgia on the old man's, the utter bliss on Brewster's, the drawing would be a perfect addition to the Washington show next month, she reflected as she got to work.

The sketch went well, her pencils flying as though guided by a talent beyond that in her skilled fingers. The excitement she saw on the young faces, the re-membrance on Uncle Zeb's wizened countenance as he gestured with gnarled hands, enhancing his words, fairly sprang onto the paper.

As she worked, Laura felt herself transported to the world of her own childhood when the old man, whom she'd grown up calling "Uncle," had regaled her with his own adventures and handed-down tales that had made the mountains seem even more magical to her.

Some of the stories, she mused, as her pencil skimmed the sketch paper, deftly shading, might even have been true. But it hadn't mattered whether they were or not; they had fired her imagination.

Beside Joanie, Brewster suddenly picked himself up from his totally relaxed bearskin-rug sprawl. Yawning, stretching, plume waving, the dog looked expec-tantly toward the point where the narrow road that passed in front of the store disappeared around a wall of jagged rock that thrust out from the tree-covered mountainside. The sun's last rays before it dropped behind the mountain gave the rough stone the sheen of gray velvet in the softly romantic light.

"Hey!" Eddie shrieked, bouncing to his bare feet. "It's Glen's Buick!"

For a five-year-old, he possessed what Laura considered an astounding knowledge of cars; like his father, she often had thought with a spurt of sadness. He made the exuberant announcement as the car's hood ornament appeared around the treacherous elbow turn that lay beyond the "giant's shoulder," as one of Uncle Zeb's stories described the jutting layers of stone.

Laura's heart missed a beat and then leaped to catch up with itself. Glen had called right after he'd left the hospital yesterday saying he had "a few things to do" and that he would see her "in two or three days." Pretty indefinite, she had thought, then, with a vague stir of apprehension.

Now, feeling as though she'd been handed the first present off the Christmas tree, Laura folded the cover over the drawing she'd been working on and stood up.

All was suddenly right with her world: Glen was back.

"Don't know who's gladdest," Uncle Zeb grumbled, half under his breath, watching the kids and Brewster dance and prance around Glen as he climbed stiffly out of the car. "Them young'uns and that dog, or Glen."

Impulsively patting his bald spot fringed with thin, iron-gray hair, Laura had the feeling Zeb had intercepted the glance that had passed between her and Glen over the children's heads. Uncle Zeb might be nearing ninety, but he didn't miss much, especially where she was concerned. She loved him dearly for it.

Carefully she placed the sketch pad and the handful of drawing pencils on a chair beside Uncle Zeb's rocker, using the moment to regroup her senses. She'd never felt so loved and loving in her life, and she wasn't quite sure how to handle the sensations now.

How did Glen *really* feel about her?

Because she wanted so much for him to love her, was she reading more into that one intense look than had been there? Had she read more into that evening at her little house up the mountain than had been there? Had they merely been caught up, that evening, in the magic of the dusk settling over the mountains and into their souls?

Had Glen, on that lyrical evening, truly meant it when he'd whispered against her hair "I could stay like this forever"? Or had they both been carried away by emotions neither of them was ready to deal with?

"Laura."

She hadn't known he could move so fast, but suddenly his hands spanned her waist—and then moved, gently caressing, up to her shoulders.

When he turned her into his arms, she went as naturally as though they had rehearsed many times; as though the grim specter of his return to Marazán weren't between them.

"I'm glad you're back," she whispered huskily, her face lifted to his. And she realized her lips had forgotten to close.

"Glad to be back."

His lips brushed hers, nibbled hungrily while his tongue probed tentatively.

"Aunt Laura's got a boyfriend! Aunt Laura's—"

One of Laura's hands reluctantly left its thoroughly contented position, palm pressed to Glen's chest, and covered the child's chanting mouth.

"—got a boyfriend!" Eddie singsonged against her muffling palm.

Suddenly warm all over, Laura lifted her eyes to meet Glen's and saw silent laughter. Warmed by the look and by his breath fanning out hot and moist and seductive against her skin, she couldn't help smiling back.

"Aunt Laura's—"

"That's enough, Eddie," Laura warned, trying to sound stern as she stepped away from Glen.

The added space between them didn't do a thing for her composure. Her blood still raced too warm through her vessels, and her breathing continued too fast and shallow to supply her lungs with the oxygen they needed to steady her runaway heart.

And if Joanie didn't stop looking at her like that— as though she'd just discovered every little girl's dream of romance and that Glen and *she*, Laura Crane, were its flesh-and-blood embodiment—she would melt down at Glen's feet.

"Joanie," she began in desperation, "don't you and Eddie have to be home before dark?"

It was no problem, really. Their grandparents' farm was less than half a mile from the store, and if they weren't home by suppertime, Johnny Lewellyn, their young uncle, would come for them in his pickup. It had happened at least three nights a week since their mother's return to Atlanta, leaving them to spend the rest of the summer.

With a look that was wise beyond her seven years, Joanie caught her younger brother's hand and whispered something in his ear. Eddie promptly looked excited enough to burst his buttons.

Impulsively Laura kissed them both.

"See you tomorrow," she promised. "Don't forget, we've got a picnic to go to."

"Can Glen come, too?" Joanie sounded eager.

"Hey, yeah!" Eddie squealed his excited support of the idea.

Smiling, Laura said, "If he wants to."

If he didn't want to, she thought, she would be more disappointed than the children.

"What was that about a picnic tomorrow?" Glen asked when he and Laura had finished carrying into the cabin the books and clothing and other things he had brought from his apartment in Washington.

The car, Laura had noted with a rush of hope that he wasn't in a hurry to put Crane—and her—behind him, had been loaded for bear.

Now, they were seated on the deck, waiting for a fryer to bake in the oven. She had already made a green salad from things she'd brought down from the store and her grandfather's garden, and brewed a pot of coffee. Empty mugs sat on the deck beside them.

Dusk had settled into darkness. A tranquillity that Laura had grown up accepting as a part of the Cumberlands' magical therapy for wounded spirits touched the lake and the mountains that surrounded it.

The only sounds she heard were the far-off baying of Johnny Lewellyn's hounds running a raccoon, and the occasional cry of a lonely whippoorwill. Off across the lake were lights from another of her grandfather's carefully isolated vacationers' cabins, reminding her that she and Glen weren't the only two people in the world.

After hearing some of the things he told her he'd learned during his time in Washington, she almost wished that they were, although she could have hugged John Baz—whom she'd never met or even talked to on the phone—for suggesting Carlos Rodríguez for the Marazán assignment. She hoped the editor stuck to his guns, no matter how disappointed and probably angry Glen would be.

"The Lewellyns' church—you've seen it up the road—is having its annual summer picnic tomorrow. Auntie Liz, the kids' grandmother, asked me to help her ride herd on them."

She sensed Glen's slow grin in the darkness. "Sounds like one smart lady."

A responding smile lifted the corners of Laura's mouth. "She raised their father and three others and helped raise me, after Mama died. You could say she learned the hard way what mischief kids their ages can get into even at a church picnic."

"How old were you?"

With the low-voiced question, his hand sought hers as they sat on the rustic bench. It was the first time he had touched her since the brief caress at the store. Laura's pulses quickened in response.

"When your mother died," he added when she didn't speak at once, although she'd known what he had meant.

As if of its own accord, Laura felt her other hand close over his. Her fingers linked with his, and she could have sworn she felt his caring and sensitivity pass from his hands into hers—and flow through her body.

Glen might not love her as she loved him, but he cared for her—deeply. She felt it.

"Not quite two." She drew a breath of the cool, soothing night air deep into her lungs. "Sometimes...sometimes I think I remember her...remember it happening, although I know I couldn't possibly."

"You don't have to talk about it, love."

She went on as though she hadn't heard him, wanting to tell him, wanting so much to share that part of her life with him. "Daddy was a training officer at Fort Benning. Mama was driving to the base to pick him up. I was in the back seat, playing with my doll, which probably saved my life.

"The...police told Daddy she was...driving too fast."

Swallowing hard, she paused, her throat achy. How could she hurt so badly when she'd never really known her mother?

"Daddy resigned his commission when his enlistment was up—he'd been a career officer—and brought me home, to Crane's Mountain. We lived behind the store, he and Grandpa and my grandmother till she died. When the Vietnam War came, he reenlisted.''

She hadn't known when Glen's arms had gone around her shoulders and he had drawn her head against his chest. But her cheek was pressed against the rapid pounding of his heart, his face buried in her hair....

Chapter Nine

"I could stay like this forever." Recalling Glen's words to the same effect, she felt as though she were melting inside, as though she and Glen had been poured into the same mold and would emerge as the personification of a man and a woman passionately in love.

Where had that image come from? Laura wondered. She was an artist with brush and pencil who worked on canvas and sketch pad, not one who painted pictures with words. Glen was the one who did that.

Was he experiencing the same tempest of sensations that was sweeping through her? Having the same visions that had sent her imagination soaring toward the very edge of the universe? Dear heaven, she felt ready to explode like some distant nova.

"Glen," she whispered, scarcely believing the heated emotions that rushed through her.

Her lips brushed the rough fabric of his blue shirt—and became as sensitized by the contact as if they had touched his naked flesh.

Ever so gently Glen lifted her face and kissed her, her temple first and then her lips. His tender caresses incited a renewed surge of pleasure that raced unbridled through her.

Lips and teeth nibbled, nipped; his tongue probed gently, begging an invitation to enter her mouth and taste her sweetness. She couldn't have resisted even if she had wanted to. Her lips parted, letting her senses feast on the exotic essence that, she told herself, was his and his alone.

Lifting his mouth abruptly from hers, he asked hoarsely, "Do I detect a but in there somewhere?"

I didn't intend to fall in love with you.

Why couldn't she tell him? Why couldn't she utter the words flat out: I didn't want to love another man who will put his life on the line for something he believes in—an ideal he has already risked his life for—without thinking of me first? Without putting me first?

Before she knew what was happening, Glen would be off to Marazán, leaving her to wait and wonder and worry if he was alive—or whether he would be coming back at all; and maybe to hear on another television-news program, as she had first heard the news about Frank, that the man she loved had been killed.

"No—" Her voice, answering the question, ached with longing she couldn't, in her heart, deny. "But—"

His mouth came down again, silencing her, claiming the kiss she offered on her slightly parted lips.

Other than the tender capture and the exquisite surrender of her mouth, she had scarcely been aware of their movements. But she was cradled in his arms, her palms flattened against his chest as she lay across his lap.

Through the thin fabric of his shirt she felt the fine sprinkling of crisp hair. His heart pounded out a fast rhythm against one of her palms, echoing the quickening beat of her own. Mind and body, she felt herself responding to his unspoken plea.

Although they were on the narrow bench Johnny Lewellyn had hewed out of one piece of a huge, storm-downed oak tree three winters before, Laura had never felt so comfortable or so safe—when nothing could be further from the truth: Glen would go, and he might not come back.

She had been a fool to let herself fall in love again.

A sigh escaped her. It was too late for such self-recriminations; far too late, she realized with the remote fragment of her being that still clung to the barricades she had flung up around her heart. Every shred of her body wanted to love him—to know his love for her—not only now, but for the rest of her life.

How could she *not* tell him?

One slender hand had abandoned its safe harbor against Glen's chest and now was at his nape. Splayed fingers urgently thrust into the unruly forest of short black hair, cupped the back of his head, sought to press him deeper into the kiss.

Oh, Glen, don't stop! she pleaded silently when she sensed him about to pull away from her. She began to kiss him back, instinctively catching his bottom lip between her teeth.

The nip, playful, teasing, came from the primal depths of her soul, releasing a burst of desire that frightened her. She hadn't known she was capable of such explosive passion, such yearning.

Inside the cabin the oven timer dinged.

In the intensity of the moment, the lilting little sound announcing that the chicken for their meal was ready rang out like a claxon.

The moment she'd begun kissing him back had very nearly been his undoing, Glen reflected later. When she had drawn his bottom lip between her teeth and then had touched the imprint her teeth had left on its sensitive inside with the tip of her tongue—testing, titillating, whetting his appetite for her, whether that was what she intended or not—he'd almost lost his grip on reality.

God, he had wanted more of her than her mouth. He'd wanted all of her.

With an agility that surprised him despite the progress he knew he had made during these past weeks of Crane's Cumberland Mountain Magic Therapy, Glen got up off the mattress he had dragged off the bottom bunk-bed during his first night in the cabin and pulled on his pants.

Short bunk or not, it wasn't a night for sleeping, that was for sure—not for him.

It hadn't been the timer's fault, and he didn't think it had been Laura's. Judging by the way she had kissed him—the sweet, languorous way she'd returned his kiss—his guess was that she had been as ready as he to make love. She may even have wanted it as badly as he, although he couldn't imagine that. He still ached.

"So, come off it, Moran," he muttered, scarcely aloud, his voice resembling the harsh call of a night bird in the darkness. "You've got to get your priorities straight. Get Marazán behind you."

That was getting his priorities straight? When what he wanted most was Laura in his life, to make a home with her, have children with her?

When had he started thinking along those lines?

As if he didn't know, he mused. Seeing his sister Laini's new happiness, becoming aware of her sense of fulfillment, her sense that now she had it all; realizing that D.J., who'd been as caught up in the Washington rat race as he, had found a new life for himself in Sycamore Point, with Laini, had woken him up to what he was missing in his own life. Laura, he reminded himself, hadn't been in the picture then, except as a name, as part of the promise he had made to Carrera.

Since he'd met her, the emptiness in his life had hit him like a ton of bricks.

Swearing under his breath, he strode out of the cabin's tiny bedroom to the kitchen alcove where he heated up the coffee left over from supper.

As he poured himself a brimming mugful, he swore to himself that he wouldn't let himself picture Laura as she had measured out the coffee, filled the percolator from the faucet that carried spring water to the cabin from higher up the mountain, sat across the table from him as they'd eaten their oven-fried chicken and the salad.

In his mind's eye he saw her do all those things again—and more, some of them only in his inflamed imagination.

Although she had left right after supper, Laura was still with him. Her sweet scent still filled his nostrils and his lungs although a light breeze blew through the cabin's open windows and door, bringing with it the smell of the lake's freshness and the mysterious fragrances that came from off the mountain.

After gulping his coffee, Glen fled Laura's bewitching enchantment in the only way he knew how: shoving an empty disk into the computer, he got to work on the idea that had been with him since he'd talked with Baz before he left Washington.

The first words on the screen were "The Conscience of Marazán: The Story Of Juan Hernández And Of Isabelle, The Woman Who Inherited His Mantle."

He was still at it when dawn broke, pearl-toned and then pink and crimson, over the mountains. Johnny Lewellyn's hound-dog pup, which had taken to dropping by as though it recognized a kindred spirit, whined at the screen door.

Yawning, Glen stopped keyboarding and went outside for his morning run along the lake, with the dog oping companionably at his side, reminding him poignantly of Fruitful, the old hound he'd taken in, and Murphy's speckled pup back at Sycamore Point. Both dogs and the boy had walked with him, often ranging far afield but always bounding back, their excitement and affection overflowing. He missed them all.

"I hope Jo finds a nice young man like your Mr. Moran," Elizabeth Lewellyn confided to Laura the next day as they sat at one of the tables.

The picnic lunch had been spread on tables set up in the grove of hickory, oak and maple trees that surrounded the small, white, tall-steepled church. In an adjacent meadow, assorted games now were under way and would continue, to the tune of shouts and hoots, until the small crowd broke up late in the afternoon. An impromptu songfest—she hadn't heard a church song yet, Laura thought with a secret smile—had broken out.

Glen was on the improvised softball field, attempting to show Eddie and a group of other youngsters how to throw a curveball.

Smiling, Laura replied, "He isn't *my* Mr. Moran, Auntie Liz."

The older woman shook her head, laughing softly as she ran fingers that were becoming gnarled with arthritis through her graying hair. "I saw the way he looks at you, the way you look at him. The way you've been watching him out there with the young ones, taking in every move he makes."

Laura started to protest but decided against it. She never had been able to fool Auntie Liz. She decided, instead, to change the subject—sort of.

"I'm surprised you'd say Jo needs a man in her life, Auntie Liz. You know how she felt about Eddie." And *she* knew how Auntie Liz had felt about her eldest son.

She wondered if Jo had let her late husband's mother know how bitter she'd been about the reckless determination to win that had been the cause of Eddie's accident on the track; and how Jo had declared herself determined never to love a man who had a streak of adventure in his soul. Eddie Lewellyn had eaten, slept and breathed excitement, but his widow, Lord love her, seemed to have forgotten that those were the characteristics that had made him the man she'd fallen in love with; the man who had given her eight wonderful years of marriage and the two children she adored.

But then, was *she*, by promising herself to let her relationship with Glen go no further, robbing herself—and Glen—of a chance at what Jo and Eddie had shared, for however short a time?

She'd never known two happier people than Jo and Eddie Lewellyn, and she suspected that Jo, for all her grief and her proclaiming she wouldn't marry another adventure-loving man, would never trade those eight years with Eddie for any treasure in the world—nor forget them.

Think about it, Laura Crane, her other self—the self that was usually right—advised.

Slowly Elizabeth Lewellyn rocked back and forth on the bench, her gaze focused on the playing field where

Glen had drawn his right arm back to demonstrate how the softball in his hand should be thrown. Laura forgot to breathe as she watched.

"Jo and Eddie had a good marriage," Elizabeth began, her tone soft, the words sounding so far away that Laura realized her Auntie Liz was living in the past, for the moment, anyway. "But Eddie's gone, and his children need a man they can look up to.

"Look at young Eddie and Mr. Moran out there now." A sigh quivered past Elizabeth Lewellyn's lips. "Joanie's the same way. Every third breath they're talking about him."

On a warm impulse Laura clasped the other woman's work-hardened hands in both of hers. "Much as I love the kids and Jo and you, Auntie Liz, they can't have him."

Leaning over, she kissed the older woman on one sun-bronzed cheek. Now, why had she said what she had? She had a lot of thinking to do.

She and Glen had a lot of talking ahead of them before she was willing to commit to anything more than friendship. Which she fervently hoped they would always share.

But she wasn't sure she wanted Auntie Liz doing everything in her not inconsiderable power to get Glen and Jo together. Look how Auntie Liz had been, Laura found herself thinking, remembering, when she and Eddie had casually dated for a while: Auntie Liz had worked on them, certain they had been "meant for each other," until the day Eddie had slipped his ring on Jo's finger.

Freeing her hands, Elizabeth Lewellyn patted one of Laura's. "The Lord works in mysterious ways, honey."

With an irreverent grin, Laura teased lightly, "What does that have to do with Eddie and Joanie wanting Glen to marry their mother?"

Auntie Liz gave her hands another squeeze. "Who said anything about Jo and Glen? It's you and Glen the Good Lord brought together, honey. It's the two of you who were made for each other, as anybody with eyes in his head can see plain as day."

At the pitcher's mound, Eddie, under Glen's tutelage, wound up for a mighty pitch.

Watching, Laura smiled to herself as the ball went just about as wild as a ball pitched by a five-year-old could go. Glen, dropping to his good knee beside Eddie, caught it after a boy chased it down and threw it back to the plate.

Anybody with eyes in her head, Laura thought, borrowing the phrase from the older woman who sat beside her, could see how wonderful Glen was with kids. No wonder Eddie and Joanie were so enchanted with him.

No wonder *she* was.

"Granddaughter—"

Laura started at the low boom of her grandfather's voice. Glancing over her shoulder, she saw him getting out of his ancient sedan at the edge of the picnic ground behind the church.

"Run over and tell Glen Mr. Baz called him from Washington." He finished the sentence as he drew near the bench where she and Elizabeth Lewellyn still were seated. "Wants Glen to call back soon as possible. Tell him he can ride back to the store with me if he has a mind to."

Her heart sinking, Laura rose and jogged toward the meadow where the games—the noisiest a game of horseshoes, with a dozen men on one team cheering a ringer while members of the other team groaned and hooted—were in progress.

What was it this time? she wondered. The editor's calls, especially those that required a quick callback, usually meant bad news from Marazán. And this time—after what Glen had told her last night—she feared the worst. Any word about Isabelle Hernández was bound to send Glen deeper into his preoccupation with the troubled Central American country.

"Hey, Aunt Laura!" Eddie Lewellyn squealed, greeting her excitedly. "Watch me!"

The ball left his pudgy young hand, wobbling noticeably in the air between pitcher and waiting, poised bat.

"Good pitch!" Laura applauded.

Glen caught the returned ball as he listened to her relay the message from her grandfather, then handed the dirt-smudged softball to her. "Want to take over here?"

She started to say no, not really, then didn't. He didn't want her with him when he talked to Baz about Isabelle Hernández, she guessed.

And she had promised Auntie Liz to help keep an eye on Eddie and Joanie till the picnic wrapped up. Joanie seemed to have disappeared along with the gaggle of giggling young girls she'd been with a while ago as they'd watched two or three boys their age play one-on-one at the basketball goal. A quick glance told her the boys were still shooting baskets, and she relaxed.

"Sure," she agreed, smiling at Glen. "Did I tell you I'm a pretty darn good pitcher?"

"Bet you are," he said, and winked at Eddie who winked back, screwing up one whole cheek in the process.

Walking past Laura, he brushed a kiss casually across her temple. "See you back at the ranch," he said, his voice a low, raspy rumble, for all the world as if they had something going between them, Laura thought in spite of herself.

If only they did!

If only she dared let it happen.

Chapter Ten

The couple of days that Laura had planned to be in Washington completing arrangements for her one-woman show of wildlife paintings and sketches had stretched into nearly a week.

Now, driving her Cherokee, which she had left in a parking area at the Louisville airport during her absence, she could scarcely wait to get home to start putting the exhibit together, and to add the finishing touches to another painting she had done of the Vietnam Veterans Memorial—this time with Frank's face superimposed against the sky—that she planned to send to Carmelita, Frank's sister.

Who are you trying to fool? her other self demanded derisively. You know why you're driving like a crazy woman over these mountain roads, and it isn't to put together a collection of drawings, watercolors and oils showing wildlife of the Cumberlands in its natural habitat. And it isn't to complete the painting that's your farewell to whatever it was you had with Frank Carrera—you can't wait to see Glen...hear his voice...hold him....

She might even tell him how much she had missed him, how much she loved him, *wanted* to love him— but was determined not to?

Falling in love with Glen Moran meant almost certain heartbreak. Without doubt, it meant the kind of worry that could drive a woman mad when he was off in some place like the Middle East or Marazán.

Although she knew it was too late—that she already was deeply in love with him—she vowed, again, not to let it happen to her. She *couldn't* let herself love him! It would hurt too much if she lost him.

Sighing, she wondered how she could tell Glen that. How could she make him understand her feelings without hurting him?

Feeling light and airy in her Cherokee, the way a hawk riding a thermal appeared from the ground, Laura rocketed along behind the stream of cars, homeward bound in a burst of happy anticipation in spite of her troubled thoughts.

Oh, Glen, it's going to be so good to see you!

Since it was Saturday, Laura wasn't surprised to see Jo's snazzy little sports car parked beside the store's gasoline pump. Jo frequently drove up from Atlanta to spend weekends at the farm.

Jo, who was filling the tank herself, looked around when she heard the Jeep and waved.

"Hi!" Laura called out as she stopped the Cherokee near the steps to the store's front porch.

"Hi, yourself." Jo returned the greeting as she topped off the tank and hung the hose back on the pump. "Uncle Mason said you might be coming home today."

Taking the keys from the ignition, Laura collected her shoulder bag and carryon from the seat beside her. As she climbed out of the Jeep, she glanced around for Eddie and Joanie, for whom she had presents. She didn't see Brewster, either, which, she thought, probably meant that kids and dog were down at Glen's cabin on the lake or off somewhere walking with him, exploring the mountain trails she knew like the back of her hand.

"Are the kids down at Glen's?"

"I doubt it, since Glen isn't there."

Laura stopped in her tracks.

"Where are they?" Something in Jo's tone bothered her. "Where's Glen?"

"The kids went with Johnny to get watermelons over by Lanier."

Before she continued, Jo got in her car and drove it a few feet from the gasoline pump although Laura doubted another customer would arrive within the next few minutes. The pump didn't do all that much business. Which, she thought testily, Jo knew perfectly well. So Jo was dawdling over her answer.

"I don't know where Glen is," Jo admitted finally as she got out of her car and came back to where Laura waited. "The kids were complaining when I got here last night that he had left yesterday afternoon when—" she giggled "—they had expected to go on monopolizing his time for the rest of the day.

"If Uncle Mason knows where he went," she added, "he isn't saying."

Her grandfather wouldn't, Laura knew. In his eyes, a man's business was his own.

But she turned on her heel and marched up the steps and into the store, with little more than a "Hi, Uncle Zeb" as she passed the old man who half dozed in his favorite chair. She felt betrayed. Glen should have been here when she returned. There was so much she wanted—no, *needed*—to tell him; so much she needed to hear from him, like, she thought, what he had decided about Marazán. The last she had heard, Glen's editor had been leaning toward sending Carlos Rodríguez in Glen's place, and Glen had been furious.

"Grandpa—" Coming up behind him, she leaned over his shoulder as he sat at his desk and kissed his cheek. "Did Glen say where he was going?"

"No, honey, he didn't."

"Or when he'll be back?"

"That neither."

Laura's heart, already heavy, plummeted. If he'd gone to Marazán without talking to her, without saying goodbye, what did that tell her?

"Don't worry, honey," her grandfather said when she didn't speak. "He'll be back. You can bank on that."

"Can I, Grandpa?"

Lord love him, if he *had* gone to Marazán, she hoped he was all right; would be all right.

If he wasn't, if anything happened to him, she reflected, feeling a sense of panic begin to stir, Lord love *her*.

She found her voice, finally. "Did he talk with John Baz before he left?" The words sounded thin and strained, fearful, in her own ears. Glen's Washington editor was more bad news than good, where her peace of mind was concerned.

Without speaking, her grandfather reached into one of the pigeonholes of the rolltop desk and brought out an envelope. "He left this for you," he replied as he handed it to her, his eyes twinkling with understanding. "I expect maybe it'll tell you what you're dying to find out."

Pulses pounding, Laura ripped open the envelope on which Glen had scrawled her name. The rock steadiness she'd always prided herself on maintaining no matter what the circumstances, seemed to have deserted her. They rarely did, but now her hands shook as she drew the folded sheet of computer printout paper from the envelope.

Love— Glen had written in his usual sprawling scrawl. That wonderful word again.

Isabelle Hernández called from Miami. She's ready to talk about the book.

What book? Laura wondered. Not the one Glen had been working on earlier; it had been about Murphy— a small lost boy's odyssey as he'd searched for the home and family he'd finally found in Sycamore Point.

I'll miss you, Glen's note continued. *Luck getting ready for your show. See you in a month or so. Glen.*

P.S. There're three young squirrels in the thicket behind the cabin that can use a friend. That crazy hound pup of Johnny's brought them in the other day, one at a time, like an old cat carrying her kittens.

*Guess some hunter got the mother. Something tells me
Johnny's got a problem if he's expecting to make a
hunter out of that pup.*

Well, at least, Laura mused, smiling at the last sentence, he'd called her his love—again.

It was beginning to look as though that was all she'd
ever hear from him.

Isabelle Hernández emerged from the house in Miami where Glen had been told he would find her.

On the patio, Glen waited, walking up and down
beside the pool because he was too stiff and tired from
the long drive down from Kentucky to do anything
else.

"Glen—"

Both her hands reached for his as she came toward
him, a portrait of elegance he had trouble associating
with her violence-torn country.

"It's good to see you again."

Catching her hands in his, Glen squeezed them
warmly. "It's good to see *you*, Isabelle. Believe me,
it's good to see you."

He shook his head at her, feeling a recurring rush of
the vast relief he had felt when he'd heard her voice on
the phone in Mason Crane's store.

"You gave me a scare—gave all of us a scare. How
the heck did you get out?"

Isabelle's beautiful face twisted into a pretty grimace. "It wasn't easy, either to leave Mother Hernández or my country. Or to reach the border. But I
had to do it, Glen. Mother Hernández and I agreed
that it was the only way. Juan would have wanted me

to carry on the fight, which I could not do if I stayed in Marazán City."

She paused for a moment, then continued. "There had been threats against the children and against me. My life—yes, I could and would risk it gladly. But not the lives of the children. There seemed nothing else I could do. Here in the United States, perhaps I can rally support for my people as I could not do in Marazán."

"What about Señora Hernández?" Glen asked.

An expression of regret swept over Isabelle's lovely face. "She will be safe in the consulate—she has been granted asylum—but I shall miss her. The children already miss their *abuela*." The wistfulness in her tone told Glen that she, too, already missed the children's grandmother.

"She refused to leave Marazán," Isabelle continued with a sigh. "But I think what she really wanted was to be certain that the children and I had that little extra protection her story to the authorities provided—that little extra time to make our escape."

"How did you manage that?" Glen asked, finally seating himself on one of the rattan chairs by the pool. He had felt uncomfortable pacing up and down, stretching his tortured muscles, while she sat as still as a sculpture of a Spanish lady in repose.

Isabelle waved a ringless hand in a gesture that could only be described as airy—a hand that Glen had seen raised and clenched into a fist as she had stood beside her husband when he'd spoken out at rallies protesting the corruption in Marazán.

"I took the children for drives in the country. We did it for several days, always following the same route. On the day that we actually left, we left everything behind, except for one toy each for the children—things they usually carried to amuse themselves as we drove in the country, small toys that would appear a natural thing for children bored with riding in a car to have along."

A faint smile crossed her face. "On the day of our escape, as planned, friends among the guerrillas waited for us at the river crossing. We traveled downriver lying in the bottom of a boat that stank from yesterday's fish. We were hidden under vegetables freshly dug for sale at the markets in the city. On top of us was a layer of rushes to keep us from view while the produce was being unloaded at the marketplace and as the boat made its way on downstream."

A delicate shiver, scarcely visible, swept over her. "I have never known such a conglomeration of odors nor been so frightened in my life as we lay under those rushes while the boat was being unloaded. The children thought it a great adventure."

Her dark-eyed gaze sought his, and she continued. "I should not be telling you all this, Glen, as though I should have your applause for having survived an ordeal. Juan told me how he found you lying near death in that hut in the jungle and what you had gone through in your effort to help our people—to tell the sad story of our country to the world outside. I have survived nothing by comparison."

Glen dragged in a breath of air that was heavy with the exotic perfumes of the brilliant tropical flowers filling the patio. To him their scent didn't compare with the aroma that he had smelled in the Cumberlands—especially those elusive fragrances off the mountain when they mingled with the sweet essence of Laura in his arms and in his dreams.

"Then he *was* there." He spoke matter-of-factly—much more matter-of-factly than he felt at the moment. "I thought I'd heard his voice, thought I had seen that handsome black beard of his."

Shaking his head, he continued. "But I was lost in a fog, sort of floating in and out of consciousness. I couldn't be sure. Then the guerrillas carried me to a hospital and by the time I could ask questions, I was back in the States."

Isabelle nodded, then said, "Juan had been at the mission that day. He had heard of the plane crash a few days before and had gone out with a reporter and a photographer from the paper because the territory was considered very dangerous. My husband, may God rest his courageous soul, felt that his presence might protect the people who worked for his newspaper."

After a pause, Glen guessed, to collect herself, she continued. "While he was at the mission, someone told him there had been a call from the States—Frank Carrera's fiancée. She had been near hysteria, poor woman, because she had heard the news on the television and no one would tell her what had happened."

An image of Laura flashed into his mind.

"The people at the mission were terrified of General Mariana's men, who were still in the area," Isabelle said. "Two or three soldiers were in the mission at the time Juan was there, and it was feared that if they learned of the call, they would burn the mission because they would be certain the mission was hiding you."

Glen took a deep breath.

"Juan said the soldiers knew you had survived the initial impact and the explosion. Your body had not been found. They were still searching for you. As Juan was leaving the mission, one of the *trabajadores* whispered to him that he knew where you were and would take Juan there."

"Lucky for me."

"*Sí.*" Except for *trabajadores* and *abuela*, it was the first time Isabelle had slipped into her native tongue. Educated at private schools in Marazán and then at Radcliffe, where she had been a student when she had met and married Juan Hernández, she sounded as American as he, Glen thought.

Her black eyes clouded. "But not the poor *mestizos* who had sheltered you, I am afraid. They sent the two young guerrillas off with you on the litter, then they waited too long in an effort to gather up their poor possessions. Rumor was that Mariana's patrol swooped down on them before they could disappear into the jungle that might have hidden them, and that all were killed. Juan feared he may have been followed when he left the mission."

Glen felt sick to his stomach. Why hadn't Hernández told him? Those people had risked their lives for him—they might have died because of him.

And what was he doing? Wasting time that could be spent writing the Marazán story; holding out on going to Marazán himself—sneaking in, if he had to—when he knew damn well he wasn't ready, physically, for such rigorous duty, and wouldn't be for months....

* * *

"Want to go see our cave?"

"Hey, yeah, Aunt Laura!" Eddie Lewellyn chimed in on his sister's invitation. "Come see my and Joanie's cave! It's neat!"

The children had come upon Laura as she sat hunched over her sketchbook in a niche in the rocky face of a bluff overlooking a stretch of white water in the narrow stream that pitched down the mountainside toward the lake. In it she had thought herself hidden from even the piercing eyesight of the rare bald eagle that fished that stretch of the river.

But Eddie and Joanie had found her.

Closing her drawing pad and tucking her pencils into the shoulder satchel that held her supplies on her forays into "the wild," Laura grinned at them, mentally scratching the morning's work she had thought was ahead of her. The adult male eagle she had been watching for a week wouldn't dart down and snatch a fish from the frothy white water that boiled over and around midstream boulders while Eddie and Joanie literally pranced excitedly about, begging her to go see the cave she knew as well as she knew the back of her hand.

"Sure," she said, uncrossing her jeans-clad legs and climbing out of the niche.

Stretching out the kinks in her muscles from sitting still so long, she cautioned, "For goodness' sake, kids, watch your step."

The animal trail that meandered across the face of the cliff and down to safer footing for humans was treacherous enough for an adult like herself who was used to pretending she was a creature of the remote mountain. Children like Joanie and Eddie, more accustomed to city sidewalks and parks, could get into trouble *fast*.

They didn't, but for the life of her Laura couldn't understand why. Eddie, especially, ran and skipped thoughtlessly along the narrow path, swinging on bushes that looked ready to pull out of the thin, rocky soil.

Finally Laura gave up calling out to him to be careful and concentrated on making her own way along the trail—and on wishing that Glen were close behind her, or in front of her with Joanie and Eddie hanging on to his hands, instead of in Miami with Isabelle Hernández.

Although he had called two or three times, the weeks since she had held his note in her hands—and had sensed his warmth and strength and very quintessence flowing from it into her—had seemed the longest weeks of her life.

He was holding something back; she had sensed it, in his voice and in his manner.

But what? There hadn't been anything in his account of Isabelle's escape from Marazán or his conversation with "the conscience of Marazán" that affected her. And he'd told her what Isabelle had said: that although the soldiers had been at the mission at the time of her call the December before last, General Mariana had already known that Glen had been aboard Frank's plane.

So it couldn't be that, she mused; couldn't be that her hysterical near panic—her pleading with the person on the phone at the mission to tell her, to *please* tell her it hadn't been Frank's body, after all, but

Glen's that had been found—that had sent the army patrol after him.

Thank God it hadn't been she, she thought. She wasn't sure she could have lived with that. But what was behind the barely perceptible undercurrent of anger she had sensed in his tone each time they had talked? She couldn't even be sure it was directed at her; but if not at her, who else?

"Look at it!" Eddie burst out.

On his knees beside the path that had led them away from the stream, Eddie peered into a hole behind bushes and Virginia creeper he had pushed aside so she could see. With his other hand he tugged at the leg of her jeans.

"My and Joanie's very own cave!" Eddie crowed in childish glee. "Joanie says it's gonna be named after us, and everything!" He sounded ready to burst. "Want to go in and see?"

Laura smiled. As she had expected, the cave was the same shallow, high-roofed-behind-the-low-entrance cave scooped out of rock that she and Eddie and Joanie's father and their uncles had used as a "fort" to stave off imaginary Indian attacks.

"Uncle Johnny says you and our daddy played in it when you were our age. You was Becca Boone and—"

Eddie caught up his sister's rushing words. "—our daddy was Daniel!"

Impulsively she hugged both children. "We had some great old times in that cave! We really did!"

"Take care, Isabelle."

Although he knew the grounds that surrounded Isabelle Hernández's refuge were secure, guarded by hard-eyed young men who wore the marks of Marazán's rebellion with pride, Glen cast a swift, searching look around as he stood at the door saying goodbye.

"I shall," Isabelle promised.

Extending a beautifully manicured hand, she said warmly, "I look forward to working with you, Glen. My husband was right to trust you."

"There have been times when I have doubted that." Glen's hand tightened around hers. "Juan might still be alive, Isabelle, if he hadn't helped me get inside the system in Marazán and then gone on helping me after Mariana kicked me out of the country." He was thinking of the night Hernández had phoned him— and been killed less than two hours later. He suspected Isabelle was remembering, too.

Her other hand patted the back of his that grasped hers. "It was something he felt he had to do," she said softly. "Please believe that, Glen. You were our country's hope. Our country's salvation."

"I always thought Juan Hernández was that. And now you are." Leaning forward, Glen kissed her magnolia-skinned forehead. "Take care of 'the conscience of Marazán,' Isabelle." His voice was filled with the admiration he held for her.

A whip-thin guerrilla who looked as though he would have felt more at ease in the camouflage uniform he had worn in the jungles of Marazán than he did in the spiffy khaki shirt and olive-green trousers he now wore, appeared from nowhere and opened the door of Glen's Buick for him.

Thrusting out a lean, bronzed hand, the young Marazán patriot said, "Thank you for being here, Señor Moran. May God go with you."

"I should thank you for being here, amigo," Glen replied as he returned the firm handshake. He glanced toward the slight figure in white standing in the doorway. "Look out for Señora Hernández, José. She's one great lady."

The dark face burst into an appreciative smile. "She is the savior of our country, *señor*."

"She just may be that, too," Glen agreed as he climbed into the car.

Saluting, he drove off, thinking of the three weeks he had spent mapping out the book with Isabelle's help—the royalties that, they had agreed at Glen's suggestion, would go toward getting helpless children out of Marazán and educating them in the United States—and of the possibility of working with Carlos Rodríguez on the Marazán story.

Rodríguez, he reflected, reminded him of himself at that age, when he'd just been getting started as a foreign correspondent—burning with drive and ambition, filled with idealism, fired with patriotism.

And then—after all the years—he'd gone home to Sycamore Point and had seen what he was missing.

A smile plucked at the corners of his mouth and broadened into a grin as he tramped gas and pointed the Buick in the direction of Crane's Mountain.

Chapter Eleven

"You go on with your fishing plans, Grandpa," Laura told him on Saturday morning. "I need to spend the day in the store anyway, crating up pictures so I can ship them off when the UPS comes by on Monday."

By working like crazy, she had gotten ready for the show—even had some new things she was proud of.

"Saturdays can get busy," her grandfather cautioned.

Laura grinned. "Not that busy. Besides, you and Uncle Zeb haven't had a day out on the lake all summer."

"Well, if you're sure—"

"I'm sure. Want me to pack you a lunch?"

"You get on with your measuring and sawing and hammering and nailing." Laura had always made her own shipping crates and packed the pictures herself, as well as supervising the gallery hangings. "Zeb and I won't need much. Some snacks and a couple of colas apiece will do us fine. Went out and dug the worms last night."

Laura had to smile. "Wouldn't you rather use artificial lures?"

Her grandfather snorted, as she'd known he would. "Leave them for the tourists, I say. Ain't nothing catches a bass or a catfish better than worms and night crawlers."

Whistling under his breath, he set about filling the picnic basket with a thick wedge of Cheddar, a box of crackers, a jar of dill pickles from the shelf, cans of cola that Laura knew would be hung over the side of the boat in a string bag that once had held oranges, to keep them chilled. His "handy-dandy-do-everything-but-catch-the-fish" pocketknife would serve as cheese slicer, can opener and any other tool.

He was gone before she knew it.

The time passed quickly. Laura filled a small grocery order, rented a cabin for the weekend to a couple from Chicago who wanted to break up their long drive to Key West where they would spend the winter, and sawed lengths of the soft pine she used to construct shipping cartons for her paintings and sketches. She measured each carton to size for the framed picture it would hold.

Before she realized it, noon had come and gone. She made herself a ham-and-cheese on rye and took it, along with a cold cola, to the store's front porch where she sat in Uncle Zeb's rocker while she ate.

The day was blessedly serene, the blue sky filled with cotton-ball clouds that drifted lazily from west to east. The breeze was heavy with scents that were different from the fragrances of deep summer. Autumn was just around the corner, and after it would come the first sifting of snow that sometimes arrived early in the higher reaches of the Cumberlands.

Her sandwich and cola consumed, Laura leaned back and closed her eyes. She had half expected Brewster to show up while she was eating, ready for his usual afternoon snack. And the Lewellyn children, too, who hadn't missed a day all summer dropping by the store for peppermint sticks or the old-fashioned licorice whips her grandfather enjoyed handing out to children. Usually they hung around for hours.

A smile lifted the corners of her mouth. The kids and her dog were probably together, roaming the mountain.

Yawning, she thought that it was no wonder Uncle Zeb spent endless hours in this old chair. The way it seemed to caress her body, it must indeed possess some of the mountain's magic.

The sun's warmth and the faint breeze teased her face. She felt physically kissed, ever so tenderly—a gentle caress that brushed her lips and then drew away.

Her eyes flew open.

Glen!

As though it were meant to be and she had no control over the movement, her lips parted, eagerly welcoming his kiss. His mouth—his lips nibbling—felt so good on hers. And his tongue cajoled its way inside her mouth where it stroked and probed her sweet, secret recesses.

Answering the gathering strength of his arms, she pressed her body closer to his, and felt twin surges of passion—her own and his—respond. "Oh, Glen," she whispered huskily, the words muffled as they spilled into his mouth, "I've missed you so very much! I was afraid—"

"Not as much as I've missed you, love."

"—you'd gone off to Mara—"

Taking her mouth again, he deepened the kiss. Laura felt her senses sway, then soar. He did love her!

Abruptly Glen seemed to remember where they were. Laura felt the realization jolt through him, as it had, through her, before his arms loosened their hold around her.

"Eddie and Joanie generally show up when we get to just about where we were getting to," he muttered, sounding self-conscious.

Laura licked the tip of her tongue around her singing lips, tasting his kiss. "Glen—" Recapturing her own self-possession, she said, although a trifle unsteadily, "They haven't been here all day. Glen—"

"All the more reason to suspect they're probably hiding out in the trees across the road getting an eyeful." With those words, Glen's lips brushed her temple.

Laura felt the tension that had knotted in the pit of her stomach start to relax. He hadn't gone. He'd come home.

"We can always go inside," she suggested softly, feeling her body melt against his like hot wax fitting a mold. "I'm minding the store today while Grandpa and Uncle Zeb fish."

Glen's hands sliding down her arms set her on fire all over again. Delicious tremors quivered through her as, catching both her hands in his, he drew her toward the entrance.

Inside, the jangly cowbell over the door was barely silent when he dragged her against him again and his mouth descended on hers once more.

Surprised by the burst of passion when she'd always sensed restraint in him before, Laura responded as she had dreamed of doing, returning his kiss with a fervor that shook her. Blood at first rushed at millrace speed through her vessels and then turned languorous, into sweet, heated honey that seduced her senses and left her strangely, acutely, attuned to the fevered sensations that assailed her.

What had happened to Glen in Miami that he was on the verge of making passionate love with her?

As though he had sensed her unspoken question, Glen wrenched his mouth from hers.

"We have to talk." The words ground out as though through a coarse burr in his throat.

Laura's spirits, which moments before had soared to heights she hadn't experienced before, nosedived. "You're going."

No need to say back to Marazán. The inevitability that, one day soon, he would return to the tiny Central American country to finish what he had started had hung over them like a black cloud of doom to their relationship, from day one.

The fear sprinted into her mind from some recess deep in her subconscious where it had lain in hiding. In Marazán he would learn that despite what he had told her earlier, it *had* been her phone call to the mission that had sent the soldiers to the jungle hut after him; that it *could* have been her fault. Soldiers in the field on patrol might not have known he was on Frank's plane even though their general had, unless one of them had learned of her phone call.

"That's what I want to talk to you about. Baz wants to send Carlos, and for good reason. I must admit that. Carlos used to work for Juan Hernández and he has a passport." Succinctly he filled her in, telling her some things she already knew, some she did not.

"If I go with him but stop in Honduras," he hurried on, "I can make contact with the people there who help refugees flee Marazán. Isabelle is working with them, operating a kind of underground railroad that moves homeless kids from Marazán to the U.S."

He reached out to touch her face with his fingertips. "I'll be home before you know it."

Laura didn't speak, although she wanted to ask, *And what then?*

She knew how he felt, she told herself. He was driven by his sympathies, the ideals that made him the caring man that he was.

And he was haunted by the memories of people, especially of children and the things he had seen happen to them in Marazán; haunted by all the wrongs in the tiny nation that needed to be corrected.

But Glen had paid his dues. Why did he have to go, even to Honduras? The world wouldn't end if he didn't personally take on the windmills of revolt and poverty. But his world—*theirs* together—might, if he did.

Look how it had been for Frank! she wanted to scream at him. Look what *that* did to me! I don't want to endure such anguish again, Glen—I don't think I can survive it again. Not if I lose you.

But she couldn't utter the words. Instead, she pressed her face into the comfortable hollow of his shoulder and tried to let the heat of his body and his lean, hard strength reassure her.

Lord love her, why didn't it?

"I wish you wouldn't go," she whispered. "I don't want you to go."

"I have to, love," he murmured after a time, as though he had followed her thoughts down their track of torment.

His lips nuzzled through her chestnut hair to kiss her scalp. The lingering, tender caress sent sharp, tingling sensations leaping through her.

"Isabelle told me some things." His voice seemed to come from far away, from some other plane of existence than the enchanted one that was real for her only when she was with him. "I...have to check them out. Find those two kids from the jungle hut if I can. Isabelle has heard a rumor they may have survived the attack by the patrol. She thinks they may be in the refugee camp in Honduras, or waiting to cross the border."

Without lifting her face from the safe haven of his shoulder, she nodded, her cheek rubbing against the soft cotton fabric of the vivid, hibiscus-patterned shirt he had worn from Miami. Her skin felt incredibly sensitized.

He sounded so intense, so quietly angry, so holding-on-hard to the reins of his self-control, that Laura raised her head off his shoulder after a precious moment.

Shock jolted through her. His face might have been chiseled from stone: his clean-shaven jaw, with a bristle of dark beard shadowing it, was set; his lips were pressed tight; his normally warm and caring brown eyes were cold and as hard as dornicks, not softening even when they met and bored into hers.

"Glen," she whispered as her hands moved to frame his face, "what's wrong?"

Still holding her close against him, his hands moved restlessly over her back, inciting her senses even through the silken-soft knit of her shirt.

He told her.

Part of it she had heard before. Some—the part about Juan Hernández having been at the mission right after the plane had crashed, and Juan going to the jungle hut to warn of the soldiers' continued presence in the area and to see what he could do about getting Glen moved to greater safety and better medical care—she hadn't.

Glen's words struck her ears like harsh pellets of sleet or the small, hard, round snow that sometimes pelted the Cumberlands in winter when warm air from the south clashed and lost the skirmish with cold air that swept down like a Yankee invasion from the north.

A chilling dread settled into her blood. Those poor children in Marazán had haunted his nightmares. Days, he'd seen them in his mind's eye every time he looked at Eddie and Joanie and probably every other child.

Hearing the excruciating experience again, she longed to hold him forever; to more than just hold him—to make him forget, if she could, even for a short time, by giving him her love.

Now, he had to deal with the probability that they had been slain as senselessly as so many others had died in Marazán over the past twenty years of corruption, violence and rebellion.

She, she believed, had to deal with it. Regardless of what Glen had said, her panicky phone call to the mission, her begging to be told it had been Glen and not Frank who had died, *could* have added to the danger—both to Glen and to the native Marazán family that had taken him in.

There was no way he wouldn't blame her for whatever part, however small, she had played in what had happened—*might* have happened; no way he could forget that she had broken the trust Frank had placed in her when he'd told her, in confidence, that his co-pilot would be Glen Moran, who was trying to get back into Marazán to get a news story.

The thought left her numb. Her breath stuck in her throat. She was losing him—had already lost him.

"Glen," she whispered, unsure what she meant to say, or even if there was anything she *could* say.

Glen's mouth came down on hers before she could find words, let alone utter them. Her heart gave a wild lurch as his hands abandoned their gentle massage of her back and moved around her waist, slipping beneath her shirt with an urgency that seemed born of the ardent kiss.

Instinctively her arms went around his neck. One of her hands cupped the back of his head. Encouraging him, she used hands, body and hungering mouth to help him deepen the kiss.

His faintly abrasive palms ignited sparks as they moved leisurely, gently kneading the flesh over her rib cage. Her entire body felt as though it were a pillar of spreading flame about to consume her soul.

If her body hadn't functioned as nature intended, she would have forgotten how to breathe as his hands paused when they encountered the sheer fabric of her bra. And then moved to cup her breasts through the soft cotton that, suddenly, felt as though it were nothing.

She heard herself moan—a lioness's husky purr deep in her throat. Glen's responding groan excited every sense she possessed.

She almost didn't hear the jangling of the old brass cowbell over the door.

Releasing her abruptly, Glen growled something under his breath. Keeping his back to the door, he gave her the moment she needed to smooth her shirt, before he turned. There wasn't much she could do about her lips, which, she realized, tattled that she'd just been thoroughly kissed.

"Hey!" Johnny Lewellyn greeted them exuberantly, and with a brash grin that told Laura he hadn't missed much of what he'd walked in on.

"Hi, Johnny." Her voice squeaked in her own ears like a raspy old hinge. She felt as though her face were on fire.

"Johnny." Glen sounded, she thought, as though he could throttle the younger man and enjoy doing it.

Johnny gave them an impudent grin. "Came to get the kids out of your hair."

"Haven't seen them all day," Laura told him. "I think Brewster may be with them."

"Well, I hope so." Johnny's wide grin now appeared slightly worried. "Mom says they left the house early this morning." Scowling, he burst out, "Thought sure as heck they'd be here."

Laura saw the uneasiness that settled across his full-cheeked young face.

"If they've gone back to that cave they found over on Lonesome, I'll whack the tar out of both of them!" His voice sounded hollow, the threat empty.

Apprehension prickled along Laura's spine. The cave she and the Lewellyn boys had played in—the one the children had shown her—wasn't on the creek everyone called Lonesome.

The mountains were honeycombed with caves, some of them probably uncharted, even unknown; a lot of them dangerous even for skilled spelunkers.

Edging toward the door, Johnny looked genuinely worried now. "They showed it to me the other day—a real killer." He appeared scared stiff, now. "I made them promise never to go near it again—sure as heck not to venture inside."

"Let's go," Glen rasped out.

Laura's heart missed at least three beats—more than it had when she'd been in Glen's arms.

"They're in there, all right," Glen grumbled when he crawfished out of the narrow entrance, scarcely above water level on a rocky shelf at the creek's edge.

Flicking off the coon hunter's flashlight from Johnny's pickup, he stood up, wincing a time or two before he was finally upright.

"Found this." He held up a piece of peppermint candy, the kind sold at the store. It was still sticky-wet from being in a child's mouth.

"Ma will kill them two kids," Johnny muttered, shaking his head as he stared at the cave's entrance, all but hidden from view by overhanging brush. "Me, too, most likely, for not telling her about the cave when they were in it the other day."

Laura stared at the entrance. People had gone into holes in the mountain like that and never been seen or heard from again!

Or, she recollected as stories she'd heard in her childhood stalked out of her subconscious, they got hung up in a narrow fissure, or were trapped by suddenly rising water and had to be dragged out more dead than alive by men who risked their own lives to rescue them.

Her gaze leaped to Glen's face. Reading him like an open book, she cried, "Oh, no! You can't go in there, Glen!"

"Sure as hell I can't stand around here till a cave-rescue team gets here," he snapped, seeming to have forgotten that twenty minutes earlier he had been making passionate love with her. His tone cut. "Johnny, did I see a rope in your truck?"

Johnny nodded and was off like a shot.

"Laura," Glen continued, "you drive the truck back to the store. Call the sheriff and tell him everything you can about this cave. Tell him I'm going—"

"Glen, you can't! You're not— I'll go in. You go for help."

He went on as though she hadn't interrupted. "Tell him I've done some spelunking up in Indiana and in Europe. Tell him there's a good spelunking team up in Bloomington if there aren't experienced cavers closer. We may need them."

Seeming not even to pause for breath, he ordered, "Get every lantern and battery you've got in the store. Damn," he swore lustily, "I wish we could get vehicles up here! We could use their headlights when dark comes if we don't have them out by then. See if you can get an auxiliary generator or an electric line run in from somewhere," he ordered.

"Now *go*." He kissed her on the cheek.

Nodding, as she had done at each instruction, Laura felt some of her initial panic recede in the face of his take-charge strength and apparent know-how, and realized that this was the other side of Glen—the Glen who had put his life on the line time after time as he had gathered his news stories, and that he would go on doing it, no matter what happened between them; the Glen she loved and would go on loving, even if he broke her heart. She had to tell him she didn't want him to go, not even to Honduras, but that she understood why he felt he had to....

"I'll be back as soon as I can," she promised, halting her reverie.

She kissed him, whispering against his lips, "Be careful in there. I love you."

If he heard her, he gave no sign. Before she'd finished "I love you," he was on his knees in front of the treacherous little opening in the mountain. She could almost hear his brain working as he tried to figure a way to get his lean, hard body through the entrance that looked as though it had been designed, diabolically, for children only.

Clenching her teeth against another plea that he not go in there, she ran off down the path to where they had left the pickup. Johnny Lewellyn, on his way back clutching a coil of rope, passed her without speaking.

The cave was a son of a gun, Glen decided before he had moved a dozen feet from the entrance, the coon hunter's light boring into the darkness ahead of him. The rope was tied around his waist. He'd posted Johnny at the cave's entrance and instructed him to keep the rope taut and to feed it out as Glen needed to go deeper.

The roof was so low that he couldn't get off hands and knees, and crawling for him was sheer torture—and would have been torture even without the needles of rock that stuck into his palms and elbows and pierced through his jeans into his knees as he inched forward.

But Joanie and Eddie were in here; he was almost certain of it. That peppermint stick hadn't lain around for long.

Hoping the kids had a flashlight and weren't blundering around in the darkness, he aimed his own light into the passageway ahead. Checking the rope around his waist, he crawled on—cautiously. Even an experienced spelunker like himself could get into trouble in a strange cave before he knew what was happening.

"Eddie!" he called, and heard his voice echo back at him. "Joanie!"

Silence.

Except for the sound of his own voice reverberating hollowly through the blackness beyond the reach of the flashlight beam, the deadly silence scared the hell out of him.

He tried again—"Brewster!"—and uttered the keen whistle he sometimes used to summon the dog back to him when they were walking and Brewster had gone off on his own.

Nothing.

After making all the calls for rescuers and rescue equipment, Laura drove back up the mountain as fast as she dared and then, accompanied by her grandfather, scrambled over rocks and through brush along the creek.

Dusk would be falling soon. The thought of the children lost in the cave overnight sent chills skirling through Laura. She tried not to think about Glen, who was no more ready physically to tackle a "killer" Kentucky cave than he was to return to Central America, even if it would be only to Honduras.

When a wet nose touched her hand, she nearly jumped out of her skin.

"Brewster!"

The dog looked awful, bedraggled. His long black coat was matted as though it had never known a good brushing. Dropping the gear she carried, Laura threw her arms around the dog's neck and buried her face in his shaggy ruff.

"Oh, God, Brewster. Where are they? What's happened to them?"

As though he had understood every word, the big dog turned around and limped back the way he'd come, through brush that had hidden him from sight until he'd stuck his nose against her hand.

"Right with you, Brewster." Hurriedly she gathered up the tote filled with batteries and the flashlights she'd dropped, and followed.

Brewster was leading them back to the cave. When he was almost to the entrance of the cave, the dog stopped again and waited for her and her grandfather to catch up. Chocolate-brown eyes pleaded with her while he licked at a footpad that was bleeding—from being cut by a sharp rock, Laura guessed.

Laura gave him a sympathetic pat. "I wish we could stop and doctor your poor feet, Brewster."

Hanging on to her gear, she slipped and slid down the steep incline beside the dog, ending up on a shelf of rock that was hidden from above by tangled brush. How had the kids found it?

Water lapped at Johnny Lewellyn's sneakered feet as he knelt at the cave opening, hanging on to a rope.

"Any word from Glen?" she asked, dropping the bag of flashlights and batteries and kneeling beside him.

"Not ye—" Abruptly Johnny stopped speaking.

And Laura stopped breathing as Glen's deep voice rumbled inside the cave, "Get a move on, Joanie, lass! We men in your spelunking party want to get out of this blarsted cave! Don't we, Eddie, me lad?"

Giggling, Joanie came wiggling through the entrance on her stomach, into her uncle's arms.

A moment later, Laura had all three of the "cavers"—Joanie, Eddie, Glen—in her own arms, and her world couldn't have seemed brighter.

"Heroes' Hero"—Glen's Washington newspaper trumpeted in the next day's morning edition.

Laura didn't know how they'd gotten the story, with interviews and photographs so quickly, but her heart swelled with pride as she read the tear sheet Baz had express-mailed to Glen.

Fax machines were wonderful, she guessed, and undoubtedly the Lanier daily, which had covered the rescue, had one.

Glen grinned and looked embarrassed when she glanced up from the paper and said huskily, "Hi, hero."

"If there was a hero anywhere around, it's that bear you call a dog. He was with the kids when I found them, and Joanie said he'd been with them all day." His lips brushed her temple. "Bet you a nickel he would have brought them out safe and sound all by himself, soon as they'd rested and eaten their last licorice whip."

Folding her arms around his neck, Laura kissed him.

"You brought them out safe and sound, and I love you for rushing in the way you did."

"But?"

Laura sighed, feeling her heart sink deeper into the despair toward which it had been headed ever since she'd realized Glen was as determined to go to Honduras—so near to Marazán that it gave her cold shivers—as he'd been to go to Marazán, before. "You live on the edge, Glen, and apparently you thrive on it. I'm . . . not . . . sure I can do either. Even with you."

Chapter Twelve

Autumn had settled in, in earnest, by the time Laura returned home after her Washington show ended. Leaves were crimson and gold all over the Cumberlands, and some mornings, frost lay thick enough on the grass to track a rabbit.

On her first morning at home, Laura pulled on a cardigan that she could shed later in the day as the sun chased the chill out of the mountain air, and struck off with Brewster. Although she hadn't been in the city long, she needed to feel her mountain's magic in her soul, painting out the memories of noise and clamor—and the loneliness.

Isabelle Hernández, who had called frequently and who had visited the gallery while she was in Washington testifying before a congressional fact-finding committee, had telephoned in Laura's absence.

"She wants you to come to Miami, honey," her grandfather told her the moment she entered the store. "Didn't say why, but I expect it has something to do with Glen."

Glen had been gone for weeks; she hadn't heard a word from him. Although Carlos Rodríguez had filed a few heavily censored stories from Marazán City that Laura had read in the Washington newspaper, Laura felt uneasy. If anything happened to *him*, Glen would be out of Honduras and inside Marazán like a ground-to-ground missile.

Laura's heart gave a happy leap, which she promptly reined in. Glen's return from Honduras wouldn't necessarily mean the happy ending she had dreamed of, longed for, all but given up hope of finding with Glen.

Glen, she warned herself, might have other plans for his life than to spend it with her—a woman who would never be happy for long away from her mountains, who wanted a safe and serene life with Glen to love and to love her.

"You may not like what I've done, honey," her grandfather continued in his booming voice, "but I told her you'd come."

Laura threw her arms around his neck.

"Oh, Grandpa, I love you!"

Isabelle Hernández and two young Marazán guerrilla fighters—one of them the dark-eyed young man Laura had met in Washington and suspected was one of Isabelle's bodyguards—met her plane at Miami International.

"You are just in time, Laura," Isabelle said after a warm embrace. "Glen, Carlos and Mother Hernández are due to arrive within minutes."

Laura had trouble keeping her feet on the terminal floor as they hurried to the proper gate. Glen had come back safely! For a brief, exhilarating moment, it didn't matter whether it was to love her or to tell her goodbye forever. *He was alive! He was safe!* That counted most.

Although her eyes searched eagerly among the stream of passengers coming off the plane from Mexico City, she missed him—until she felt herself swept off her feet into his arms.

Without words, his mouth settled onto hers.

Finally, he spoke. "God...Laura...I've missed you." Nibbling little kisses separated the words. His heaved sigh sent a tempest of his warm, moist breath flooding her face.

"There was a time or two, love, when I thought—" He broke off abruptly, to kiss her again.

"That you'd bought the big newspaper in the sky?" Huskily she whispered the words he'd told her, once before.

"Something like that. Even though I only snuck across the border three or four times," he added as his mouth again descended hungrily on hers.

Finally, he slowly lifted his mouth away. "Love—"

It was then that Laura saw the children, about Eddie's and Joanie's ages, their black eyes solemnly taking in everything around them.

"Oh, Glen!" she cried happily. "You found them!"

"Carlos did. They've given him quite a story to go with what he kept in his head to get it past Mariana's

censors.'' A stricken expression crossed his face. ''We
couldn't leave them down there, Laura. I owe them.''

"Oh, Glen. *I* owe them." Impulsively she dropped
to her knees and opened her arms to the children.

Shyly they let go of Señora Hernández's hands. A
moment later they were in Laura's arms.

Isabelle Hernández intended to establish a home in
the United States for children orphaned by the trag-
edy that was Marazán—with Glen's help.

A few days had passed since Glen's return and
Laura's arrival in Miami, and as she listened to all the
plans, Laura had trouble seeing her role in Glen's life.
Of necessity he would work closely with both Isabelle
and Carlos. He might not be returning to Marazán,
but the tiny nation struggling to stay alive and the
book he would be writing with Isabelle, and the other
one with Carlos Rodríguez, would figure large in his
life.

Where did that leave her?

Leaning back in a rattan chair beside the pool at Isabelle's secluded home, Laura tried to focus on the
Hernández and the other children—a dozen in all and
many of them orphans—instead of on her own feelings. Glen had earned the right to live his life as he
wanted to live it, she told herself—whether that future included her or not.

She might not be happy about his choice; but she
would do everything in her power to keep herself in his
life. She knew that in her heart and soul. But . . .

Closing her eyes, she tried not to think of the plans
that might be in the making inside the house—plans
that would consume Glen if he let them. Baz had

flown down from Washington. And where Baz was, there usually was trouble for her.

Smiling to herself at the unfairness of that errant thought, she drew in a breath heavy with the fragrance of frangipani that bordered the patio. Actually, she thought she might like the man, gruff and brusque though he was. Glen, she knew, was genuinely fond of him.

"Let's go home, love." Glen's voice startled her. Her eyes popped open to find him leaning over her, about to kiss her on the lips.

"When?" she asked.

"A.S.A.P."

The hair-sprinkled backs of his long fingers caressed her cheek. Then, gently, he lifted her out of the chair and pulled her against him. With his arms folding her close, he said hoarsely, "I need to hold you and tell you—no, *show* you, how much I want and need you."

Want and *need* weren't exactly the key words she'd hoped to hear from him. "Glen," she began, and stopped, circling the wagons to protect herself from hurt.

He kissed her lightly—a feathery kiss, tender and filled with promise. "You don't know how badly I need Crane's Cumberland Mountain Magic Therapy, love. I've just told Baz I've found what I want."

With each word, his arms tightened around her, casting them body and soul in the same mold. Laura felt as though her body were fused to his, and she didn't want the feeling ever to end. She would follow—no, she would *go with* him, hand in hand—even to Marazán, if that was what he wanted and felt he must do.

With her love for him shining in her eyes and threatening to tremble through her voice, she told him that, in a husky whisper.

"And if you're homesick for Crane's Mountain, I'll never know it." Framing her face with his hands, he looked deep into her eyes. "Is that it?"

Laura managed a smile. "Something like that."

Still holding her face between his hands, he kissed her lips. "Then you better hear what I told Baz. I've found what I want. It's not chasing hard news all over the world. It's you, love. You, a family with you, all of us living on Crane's Mountain."

The twinkle was back in his brown eyes as he folded his arms around her again. "Marry me, Laura." He buried his face in the warm chestnut cascade of her hair at the soft curve of her neck. "God, how I do love you!"

Now those, Laura thought as passion exploded through her, were the key words she'd been waiting to hear. "And how I love you, Glen!" she whispered, feeling herself melting inside. "I always shall, my darling."

*   *   *   *   *

You'll flip . . . your pages won't!
Read paperbacks *hands-free* with

Book Mate · I

The perfect "mate" for all your romance paperbacks

Traveling • Vacationing • At Work • In Bed • Studying • Cooking • Eating

Perfect size for all standard paperbacks, this wonderful invention makes reading a pure pleasure! Ingenious design holds paperback books OPEN and FLAT so even wind can't ruffle pages – leaves your hands free to do other things. Reinforced, wipe-clean vinyl-covered holder flexes to let you turn pages without undoing the strap . . . supports paperbacks so well, they have the strength of hardcovers!

Pages turn WITHOUT opening the strap

SEE-THROUGH STRAP

Reinforced back stays flat

Built in bookmark

BOOK MARK

BACK COVER HOLDING STRIP

10 x 7¼ opened.
Snaps closed for easy carrying, too

OUR UNIQUE SERIES
FOR EVERY WOMAN YOU ARE . . .

Silhouette Romance®

Love, at its most tender, provocative, emotional . . . in stories that will make you laugh and cry while bringing you the magic of falling in love.

6 titles per month

Silhouette Special Edition®

Sophisticated, substantial and packed with emotion, these powerful novels of life and love will capture your imagination and steal your heart.

6 titles per month

Silhouette Desire®

Open the door to romance and passion. Humorous, emotional, compelling—yet always a believable and sensuous story—Silhouette Desire never fails to deliver on the promise of love.

6 titles per month

SILHOUETTE·INTIMATE·MOMENTS®

Enter a world of excitement, of romance heightened by suspense, adventure and the passions every woman dreams of. Let us sweep you away.

4 titles per month